The Sun's Gold

Smith Kirkpatrick

Houghton Mifflin Company Boston
1974

FIRST PRINTING V

Copyright © 1974 by Smith Kirkpatrick

Library of Congress Cataloging in Publication Data

Kirkpatrick, Smith.
  The sun's gold.

  I. Title.
PZ4.K5923Su [PS3561.1714] 813'.5'4 73-19611
ISBN 0-395-18467-3

Three selections from this book were first published in
The Sewanee Review.

Printed in the United States of America

To Andrew Lytle

. . . only a plank separates a seaman
from eternity . . .

The glorious sun
Stays in his course and plays the alchemist,
Turning with splendour of his precious eye
The meagre cloddy earth to glittering gold.

Shakespeare, KING JOHN

Contents

The Sun's Gold

S.S. Ekonk

THE STEAMSHIP *Ekonk*, fresh from six months to Africa, loaded beer, munitions, and toilet paper for another trip foreign while a new crew gathered from several nearby ports. The old crew was willing but in jail. Their first night ashore, after the hot six-month trip, the old crew couldn't find anyone else to fight so they chose up sides and fought each other. Most of the deckhands and all of the blackgang were charged with rioting, resisting arrest, disturbing the peace, and tearing up the Broken Spar Bar, whose original name was Port t' Home. Two wipers, whose duty it is to keep the engine room clean, were charged in addition with the attempted murder of a tobacco-chewing fireman who had to spit somewhere during the trip. Police found the wipers in the toilet with the fireman's head in the bowl and the tank flushing.

Another fight was now underway among lawyers and city officials over the six-month payoff. Three deckhands had missed the battle and were living in a whorehouse featuring large mirrors and a jolly madam with love tattooed on her stomach. She had already decided to loan them twenty apiece when their money was gone. Not a penny more and not that if they caused any trouble.

Cast Off

1

"BUT MY NAME *is* No Name," the slender boy said, standing his ground before the large wooden desk.

"Bull," the Steamboat Inspector said, throwing back in his swivel chair and propping his feet. "That's a lot of bull."

The brown-haired boy with brown slacks put a brown shoe on the cardboard suitcase at his feet, and with a finger he stuck the birth certificate to the desk top.

"See, it's typed right in there under name."

"Look, boy, the words 'no name' mean you weren't officially named. Lots of people don't have their names on their birth certificates, and they never know it. But you want seaman's papers."

"I've come eighteen hundred miles," the boy said. "Hitching and walking."

The Inspector jerked a thumb at a secretary rubbing her ankles together at an open filing drawer. "We're busy in here, boy."

"Not Boy, sir. No Name."

The Inspector's feet hit the floor. "Look, son —"

"No Name, sir."

The Inspector stroked the top of his bald head with both hands. "Let's start over again. What you've got here is 'no name' in quotes." The Inspector hooked his fingers beside his ears and explained that in the unlikely event the citizen's name is No Name, it is written without quotes. "But I've never seen it."

The boy's brow gathered. "Mam," he called across the Inspector's head to the secretary, "You ever make a mistake typing?"

"I sure do, boy."

"No Name, Mam."

"Sure do, No Name."

"Clare!" the Inspector said without turning his head.

The secretary banged shut the drawer and reopened it.

"All right," the Inspector said. "I'll call you 'No Name,' but only so we can talk."

"And that's without the little quotes," the boy said. "Some secretary must have mistaken my name No Name for no name and put in the quotes."

"Some dumb secretary would do just that, boss," Clare called.

"Clare!"

The drawer banged and reopened.

"I ought to know my own name," the boy said.

"It isn't only the name. We need proof you're a citizen of this country."

Astonishment spread over the boy's face. "How could I come from another country without first getting papers to leave this one?"

"Clare, come here."

She came.

"What name did he give when he first came in here and you told him he needed a birth certificate?"

Clare spread a thigh over the edge of the desk and faced the boy. "You expect me to remember the name of every stray kid comes in here wanting seaman's papers?"

"If his name is No Name, yes."

Clare studied her bare knee with a fingernail.

The Inspector held out his hand, "Give me your wallet, No Name."

The boy shook his head. "I swapped it for a hamburger when I ran out of dollars."

"Now I remember," Clare said. He *did* say it was No Name."

"Clare!"

"Honest, boss. You were out to lunch." She leaned around to face the Inspector. "And during my lunch I told Gertrude upstairs about it."

The Inspector stabbed the phone and dialed. In a few moments he patted the phone back into its cradle. "Yesterday Gertrude went on two weeks' leave," he said, looking at Clare. "I actually had to call you up here to get into this."

"She can prove it, boss. Two weeks from now she'll be back to verify every word. I didn't say anything sooner because I knew you wouldn't believe it."

"And last week I wouldn't believe North Dakota still wrote its birth certificates in longhand and used sealing wax that read Boy Scouts of America in a mirror." The Inspector took his hat from the hatrack. "Boy, don't let her sign my name. You have to be responsible for something."

After the Inspector left, the boy said, "I had to, I just had to."

"I know," Clare said. "Eighteen hundred miles is a long way without money. Why do you kids want to go to sea so much?"

The boy took from his pocket two small seashells and showed them in his palm. "Can't speak for the others, Mam, but I found out the ocean made the mountains I been living in all my life."

2

A puff of steam whistled the longshoremen from the long shady warehouses onto the loading dock. The sun pressed sap from the dock's new planks and glistened the muscles of the longshoremen. The longshoremen loaded the cargo pads and nets on the dock as checkers wrote their clipboards. The bulging nets flew the air and swung disappearing down the hatches into the belly of the *Ekonk*. In the *Ekonk*'s depths, longshoremen wrestled cases of beer, trundled thousand-pound bombs, and tossed cases of toilet paper through the air. Lights strung the 'tween deck depths where men walked with bent backs and bent knees to keep the loads from bumping the overhead. They balanced the bent loads gracefully and flipped them neatly into place. But coming back with empty muscles they walked hurt. They packed the shelves of the ship as neatly as any housewife's pantry.

On deck the steam-driven winches clattered and spurted balloons of steam hissing white and disappearing above the decks. Men shouted into the clatter, but hands said the important things. The winch drivers ran the winches to the speed of hand signals. The signalmen leaned over the hatches watching other signalmen in the ship's belly, and the loads of thousand-pounders kissed the ship's bottom. But before the shift ended a net swung wildly, and a load of beer burst on deck. Loose cans disappeared into pockets and bulging jackets. The signalmen brought the drivers their share and stacked it at their feet.

The seamen had nothing to do with the loading. It was not their job. They were not trained for it. The ship's new bosun stopped to watch the bombs dropping through the after hatch. Today was his birthday. He was seventy-four years old and had been going to sea since he was twelve. Once he had figured with a pencil and found he had spent more than fifty years of his life on deep water. He was a full-blooded German and still held German citizenship, but he sailed non-German ships, and during each of the world wars he had been sunk by German submarines.

"Big ones," he said, watching another platform of bombs. He was drinking a glass of tea one-third whiskey and was on his way to meet the First Mate.

The German language was an art lost in his head like so many other arts he had labored to learn and forgotten through disuse: sail making, ship's carpentry, what women call tatting. In his bloody days he climbed and worked aloft faster than any man he'd ever met. Sometimes when he thought of all he had done and learned and forgotten and been to and the clothes he had put on and taken off, the ships sailed and the food eaten and the words spoken, he couldn't believe one man had done it. He got tired just thinking about it.

When he was twelve years old his father bound him to the Captain of a three-masted schooner headed for the Orient. His tall father bent down and solemnly shook his hand, then handed his hand to the schooner Captain.

"He is twelve, and he is a good boy," his father said, placing a bundle of clothes on the deck.

The Captain gave him to the Cook, who felt his arms and legs and shook his head. "The potatoes will peel him."

Two years later in Australia he tied his possessions in a canvas bag and transferred to an English ship. The Englishman paid better, and there he worked the decks and sails as a seaman doing a man's work.

After doing a man's work for seven years, a ship he was on sailed into Bremerhaven, where his father had told him goodby. He helped tie the ship to the wharf, and then in the storeroom he took an ear of a hundred-pound sack of potatoes in either hand. He held the sacks straight out to his sides then went ashore.

All day he walked the streets of Bremerhaven, but it was not as he remembered. When at last he found the street where he thought he lived, it was not the street. In his sailor's gait, feet always a little apart, knees never quite locked, he walked away thinking how still the land felt beneath his feet. That night in a deep voice he sang children's songs. And that night he discovered drinking was a serious part of his life.

When he woke up aboard ship, not knowing how he got there, she was under sail for England. He was never again on a ship to Germany.

Broken rolls of toilet paper streaked the rusting deck plates. The Bosun kicked at a piece caught on his toe. Wrappings were scattered about. From each smiled the face of a little girl. The Bosun peered into the nearly full hatch. Rolls of it, boxes of it, stacks of it, all clean and white. "Shit," he said and tossed his empty glass into the river.

He had to turn sideways to lift his rheumatic legs over the foot-high coaming outside the Mate's room.

The Mate lay naked on his bunk, arms straight beside him. The Bosun tapped the open mahoghany door. The Mate didn't move or take his eyes from the overhead.

"Yes."

"I'm the new Bosun."

"Welcome aboard," the Mate said to the ceiling. "You a company bosun?"

"No."

"It's only for one trip, you know."

"I hoped for more," the Bosun said.

"She's been sold to the limeys. This is the last trip for everybody." The Mate looked briefly at the Bosun, then back to the ceiling. "Oh, I see." Then after a pause, "How old are you, Bosun?"

"Old enough. I know wood and cloth."

"My ticket reads steam or sail, too. Can you still handle men?"

"I have been Bosun thirty, forty years. I work them with my head now. It is easier."

"Easier?"

"Yes."

"An easy Bosun?"

"I do it."

"These aren't seamen. They come aboard with their gear in a bottle. When I was Bosun, first thing I did was drag out the biggest man in the focsle. Saved time and energy. If he fought, I whipped him. If he wouldn't fight, I dragged him back and got another."

"It is easy for me. Who fears an old man?"

"If they don't have fear, how will they know somebody's

running things? It's your job, but you tell the deckhands, or anybody else, I'm available. Any time."

The Mate rose from his bunk. There was little of the young man left. His body was thick and muscular with a bulging hard stomach. When he moved, the thigh muscles swung. His skin was as brown as the mahogany door and as hairless. From the neck down he was covered with tattoos. Not ordinary tattoos. These had been pricked by artists, and the Mate had planned his body like a canvas.

The Bosun had a small crude anchor on his right forearm from the one time in his life he got stewed, screwed, and tattooed, and he knew the Mate had spent years in the Orient to be so elaborately decorated. The work was all Japanese in five colors and thirty-two shades. A great flying dragon writhed up off the Mate's broad chest and disappeared over his shoulder only to curl back down the other shoulder where, over his heart, the flaming mouth and coiling tail were locked in battle. A yellow, red, and green serpent coiled out of crotch hair and joined the dragon's battle with itself. Marvelous butterflies and strange red and yellow birds with great claws flew around and in and out of the battle.

On the Mate's back the dragon became the wings of some flying creature whose wings and beak and jagged claws protected the rear. The wing tips touched down the backs of his arms and underneath the wings identical geisha girls twirled swords instead of parasols. Each arm and leg was tattooed exactly like the other. Both legs were knobby from breaks.

The Mate pulled a chair to the desk. A fly spread its wings on the Mate's right thumb and the Bosun waited for the fly to take off, but it too was a tattoo. The Bosun peeked over the chair arm to see what was tattooed on the Mate's prick.

"You know any of the new crew?" the Mate asked.

"One I sailed along of. He's asleep in the focsle. Black satchel man. Fine helmsman. You cannot tell by his wake that he ever moves the wheel."

The Bosun raised on his toes a little, but he still couldn't see it. These picture galleries, you couldn't tell what they would tattoo there. He'd seen about everything. Spotted butterflies on its head; bees ass-end-to with the stinger on the end. One he had seen with a wedding ring tattooed around it about halfway down, or up. And one had it tattooed all over in red and green and black. No other tattoo on his whole body, just that red and green and black thing hanging there like something out of Africa.

"The company'll save money this trip," the Mate was saying. "We'll do nothing that can't wait for limey hands. You ever sail regular with this company?"

"Twelve years."

"Ever hear of me?"

"I think you are the one. You have a nickname? From the Orient?"

"Yes, but don't say it."

"Aye, Mate."

"Then that's all, Bosun."

The Bosun stepped out the door.

"Tell me, Bosun. Tell me one thing since this is to be our last trip. What happens to old bosuns?"

"They die," the Bosun said.

3

The thin kid in the brown slacks went back to the focsle to wash raw egg off his hands and trousers. He licked the egg from his fingers, wishing he'd dropped one of the watermelons instead of the crate of eggs.

He would wash in the sink in the place with the lettering MESSROOM. And he would look in the refrigerator again. When he came on the ship he walked around with a piece of paper from the Agent in his hand. He tried showing the paper to the men loading the ship, but they told him to get the hell out of the way. "What are you trying to do, blow us all up!"

Then he saw a man dressed not in work clothes but an opened bathrobe with a dragon whirling on its back. He showed him the paper and found not only was the bathrobe painted but the man inside. The painted man took the paper and told him to go aft to the portside focsle where the deck crew bunked. He tried not to stare. He concentrated on watching the eyes set deep and blue in the face. But in spite of himself a red-mouthed dragon spit fire and ate its own tail in the bottom of his eyes.

"Forget it," the painted man said, shaking his head. "Come on, I'll show you."

He showed him a bed to put his cardboard suitcase on, then looked him up and down and showed him the messroom and told him about the refrigerator.

"The messboy keeps it full of cold cuts for the watches. Help yourself."

Again he opened the refrigerator and there it was. Two platters of sliced meat, all kinds. A hunk of yellow cheese as big as his head, pickles, onions, sausages, milk. Saliva hit his mouth and this time he didn't wait to build himself a sandwich and set it in a plate on the table with a glass of milk, a knife, a fork, a spoon, and a napkin. He leaned into the cool odors, stuffed his mouth, and chewed and swallowed.

But it happened again.

After four swallows it was no use. His stomach was packed. He chewed some more but spit it into the waste can and just looked. On the sideboard sat bottles of things he'd never seen. A half-full coffee urn looked five gallons. A loaf of bread with three spilling slices sat atop three unopened loaves. Four days ago his last three pennies bought three chocolate kisses. He ate one chocolate kiss one day, one the next day, and one yesterday.

He shut the refrigerator door. "I knew it would be all right," he said.

He went to check his suitcase. He stepped through the door of the focsle and stepped right back out again. He came back on it more slowly to let his nostrils dull to it. The only thing he could think of was farts turned rancid and spoiled. He eased into the room shaped like half a coffin with a double tier of bunks lining the walls. In one of the lower bunks sprawled a thin man who looked as though he had been thrown there. When he got closer, the odor got stronger. In the dim light the man's features were dark, the flesh between the trousers and the shoe was black, and he thought, Negro. Then he leaned closer. It was the dirtiest white man he had ever seen. He looked rubbed from the inside with burnt cork, and his clothes looked the same.

How was it possible to get so dirty, and he'd never smelled a worse animal. Cows and chickens and things he liked the smell of, but most of them bathed in dust or water. Even the skunk smell from the time he thought he had a rabbit in the trap wasn't so bad after he got used to it. But this.

The man moaned.

He went back outside into the clatter.

"*Look out!*"

He blinked upward into the sun.

Through the warning scream a cargo net swung wildly down. He dove beneath a ladder with his head under his arms as cases of beer broke around him.

Longshoremen were everywhere. An oily leather glove grabbed his arm.

"Goddamn stupid kid, don't you ever look where you're going?"

The glove jerked him to his feet as the longshoremen muttered and shook their heads.

"Goddamn stupid kid," the glove said. "You think because it's you stepping out it's all cleared. Stupid kids are all alike."

"I'll take him," another voice said.

The Kid turned to see an old man jerking his thumb at him. He stepped toward the thumb and onto a rolling beer can. He grabbed wildly at a longshoreman's shirt, popped a button and set off a string of curses. They shoved him across rolling cans to the old man.

"Goddamn stupid kid."

"I could have been killed," he said in the focsle.

"You are right," the grinning old man said. "Trip wouldn't be complete without a kid. How long have you been trying to catch a ship?"

"Two months."

"Here, I am your bosun. You take this two dollars and go spend it. Be back by dark. We are sailing tonight."

In his brown suit and brown-checked socks he walked the sidewalks of people thinking *I've got a job on a ship. We're going foreign on the ocean.* People began turning their heads to watch him. Some smiled and nodded. He couldn't understand it. Then he passed a mirror in a store window; he was grinning like a fool.

In a drugstore booth he drank Cokes and looked at the girls in the booths. He didn't know how to start a conversation, so he played significant titles on the jukebox. "Dreaming of You." "Waiting." "Hopefully Yours." But none of them worked. He imagined a girl's widening eyes as he told her where he was going.

He walked the streets again. In a hardware store he said he'd like to see some work gloves. The hardware man showed him a cloth pair.

"I mean *hard* work gloves."

The hardware man said, "Leather!" and slapped a pair across the counter.

Their fringed cuffs came halfway to his elbows.

"That'll be seventy-five cents."

Leaving the store, he shook his head. It wasn't right. They should have talked about them, told over how they were going with him and do the things he was to do.

Oh well.

He spent the rest of the afternoon in a thirty-cent movie watching a Western, and dusk was ankle-deep when he got back to the ship without finding a single soul to tell about his trip.

He stopped on the still hot planking of the dock. The yellow top of a taxicab floated in the middle of a long oil slick near the *Ekonk*. Crossing the gangplank among the rushing men and balloons of white steam he watched for the nets and wondered how the taxi got in the river. A load of black bombs, each with the word AMPONIC stamped in the metal, swung by. He thought he would have another look inside the refrigerator.

The messroom roared with voices, and he could hardly get inside. In an isolated circle in front of the refrigerator stood a man with arms as thick as his legs. The man's eyes were bright with anger. Briefly they met his and he was stilled by the hatred there. The man was very drunk and hammering the table with his fist.

"Try me! Anybody." He pushed toward a deckhand with thin transparent skin. "You, Gene, I know you. You're a goddamned pimp. You guys know he was raised in a Galveston whorehouse? Now he runs one. His mother was a whore, and all of his women are whores. You, Gene. You try me."

Gene laughed and drank from a bottle and laughed again. They stared at each other, and the hammering fist came down on a water glass. The arm rose with blood running down the wrist. It hit back into the broken glass without Gus changing expression.

"You're crazy, Gus." Gene said.

"Think I'm afraid of blood? Glass?" Gus hit the table again.

A man in a blue coat and khaki pants lay inside the door with his blond hair nearly under the table. Green puke dried his red tie to the steel deck. Men in cheap suits, in dungarees, in khakis, men half naked, men with billed black watch caps perched at various angles stepped and stumbled over the body. The Bosun, at the end of the table, leaned back in his chair and looked about with disinterested eyes. A quart jar of tea and rum filled the Bosun's hand. Upside-down on the table lay a policeman's hat with a stained sweatband.

"Look at it," Gus said, shaking his fist in Gene's face.

"Hey, you're shaking the blood," Gene said.

"I made it. I can spill it." The bright drops fell from several places at once and a long drop looped from the elbow.

"In or out, your blood's the same to me. But not on my shirt."

"Then move. This is not something flushed out a Galveston whore. For once in your lifetime smell *clean* blood."

Whirling and crying out a sound, Gene smashed his fist into the glass. He raised the arm, and down the white shirt-sleeve the dark stain spread like a growth. "O.K., we'll stand here pumping and see who falls."

Both stood frozen in the act of shaking his fist at the other. They swayed as though the ship was already underway. The bright blood dripped between them and pooled at their feet. Gene pulled at his bottle, watching around the side of it. Then Gus wiped his palm down Gene's face and immediately they were in each other's arms.

They lurched against the others, feet slipping in the blood. Toes were stepped on, then fists started. The men began to hit each other. The space each man filled was not to be violated. Anyone intruding was shoved or clubbed. The Kid stumbled against a man with yellowed gummy eyes. Gummy eyes struck at him, and he smelled the hand, an old hand on a glandless body.

Then he was pushed from the other side and out the door. As he stumbled backward the Bosun waved the quart jar and sang in a deep voice with closed eyes.

The Kid stepped warily out the passageway onto the deck. To his astonishment the decks were empty, the winches silent, the holds filled to the top, and the backs of the longshoremen disappearing down the dock.

And that night after the last wedge had been hammered against the battens and the last boom lashed in its collar, the Bosun and the Kid and a man called Red threw the lines off the dock bollards. Red skipped up ladders to the wheelhouse and the S.S. *Ekonk* pushed into midriver and eased off downstream between the trees.

4

The next time Red went below he would tell the Mate, *You got it. I can't kick one awake this time, I'm not coming back.*

The binnacle blurred his eyes, and he was steering by his feet. It was something new. He hadn't even known he could do it. Deliberately he closed his eyes and tried it again.

He spread his legs and set his feet. The rolls and pitches rode the ache in his bones. How long had it been now? He rang two bells the last half-hour. That meant he had been steering over six hours. His hands moved dimly over the spokes, one spoke, two.

At sea again.

He couldn't take shore anymore. A month was his limit. It frightened him the way it grew, starting in the faces, in whole busloads of faces. He had rocked his heels on the curb as the buses grunted and hissed and pumped their doors. The faces climbed down in the back, climbed up in the front. J cars, Maple Ave. Cars, 19th St. Cars, K Cars, K 19th Ave. Cars, the doors pumping them up in the front and down in the back. Not people, animals. Lines of bears stood on their hind legs wearing hats and carrying packages. Hunched behind the wheels in the cars and taxis, long-haired bears stared ahead and waited for the lights. A lioness came around the corner on her hind legs and roared in his face. He happily roared back until she ran away. The doors pumped down awkward, lumbering bears catching handrails. An old female in a falling black hat had to be shoved out growling and complaining.

He began to laugh and growl. A different kind of face stopped in front of his.

"What's the matter with you?" the Policeman said. "You better go home, fellow."

Right on course at sea.

They divided him up. They took bits and pieces of him in payment for their rooms and meals and whiskey. An hour standing at the wheel he gave the salesman for a pair of black socks. He counted it out in the white slender hands, one hour of wheel watch. The hand put the hour of him in the cash register, gave him the socks. He moved the wheel a spoke and wiggled his toes in the socks. What was the storeman doing with the used hour of wheel watch?

They would pass his minutes and hours from register to register. His bit and pieces becoming like the others, shriveled and shiny and hard and odorless.

"Hey, helmsman. Helmsman!"

The bodyless face of the Third Mate stared at him across the binnacle light.

"*You.* You were asleep."

"I was steering."

"With your eyes closed?"

"Look at it." His finger pointed down the binnacle light.

"I don't care what it says," the Mate said. "For the last fifteen minutes I've watched you sleep. You get below. I don't care if you can't wake a relief, I got it now."

"That's right, you got it." Red stepped aside, and the Mate stepped upon the steering grating and took the wheel.

"Course is one seven five, sir."

The Mate didn't answer.

"Course is one seven five, sir."

"I know what the course is."

"Steering one seven five."

"I know what we're steering. I gave it to you. You know I know the damned thing."

"It's regulations, sir. I've got to make sure my relief know's what's what. You got to say the course back to me so I'll know you got it. Steering one seven five, sir."

"That's about all I'm taking from you, Sailor."

"You steer the wrong course, and we get sand in our mouths. Course is one seven five, sir."

"Damnit, it's not bad enough I have to take the wheel because none of you damned sailors are sober enough to do your work, but I've got to listen to you give me a damned lecture about regulations. I catch you at the wheel in a sound sleep, and you worry about *me* endangering the ship."

"One seven five, and I'm off for my bunk."

"Where do they find you guys? You walk aboard for a twelve-month trip with nothing in your hands and less in your pockets. Twelve months later you walk back up the damned dock to disappear around a corner with a six-ounce ditty bag over your shoulder. Where do you go? Is there

some factory they make you guys? Been one of you scut-
tling around every damned ship I've ever sailed. Now for
Christ's sake get below."

"Not until you say one seven five so I'll know you know
it."

"You mean so you can tell them in the focsle how you
made the Third Mate say it. How you know sea law. Sea
law hell. Deck crew drunk. You been standing at the wheel
now three times longer than the legal limit and probably
couldn't see the compass if you did open your eyes. Nobody
on lookout. You and I standing here arguing right now and
not one pair of eyes watching where we're going. Sea law!
Something happens to us tonight they'll lift every ticket
here. They won't get mine. I've got a lookout up there.
The last time I went below I dragged a body from a bunk
and damned well carried him up there. He may be laying
down, and he may have his damned eyes closed, but if he
hasn't rolled over the side, I've got a lookout up there."

"Which one'd you get?"

"I didn't ask his damned name. I just got one.
Stinkingest human I ever leaned over."

"Him? Now you just give me a quick one seven five and
I'll be off, maybe I can get some sleep now I can breath the
focsle air."

"Sailor, let's get one thing straight. I'm not going to say
it, not now, not tomorrow, not ever."

The Third Mate stepped off the grating.

"Helmsman," the Third Mate said to the empty grating,
"new course. Steer one seven damned six."

The Third Mate stepped back on the grating and said
over the binnacle, "Steering one seven damned six."

They looked at each other across the binnacle. "She's all

yours, Third." At the door of the wheel house Red said back, "If I can shake one to, I'll send him up."

He went out on the wing bridge, took the railing in his hands, and set his feet. Taking deep breaths he waited for his eyes to adjust.

Tired as he was, he would like to go forward and wedge himself into the v of the bow, lean out, and forget the ship was there. With the white bone hissing and frothing at his feet he would swing and bob and slide the air to where the sea and sky met in the distance.

Nothing changed.

On the bridge the salt air got down in his throat and thighs.

At sea again.

He turned and sprang into darkness. The ladder's railing slapped his palms. His feet skipped the steps.

"Hee-hee," he said at the bottom. "Not bad for an older man."

He slid down a series of ladders and crossed a deck. The Kid stood in the dark at a low chain railing.

"You," he said. "You oughtn't do that."

The Kid turned, startled. "I thought I was alone."

The face of the Kid was loose with fright and young as a bird's.

"Oughtn't stand that way."

"What way?"

"See how I'm standing? See my hand?"

The Kid looked at Red's hands: one at his side, one at the chain railing.

"Don't ever," Red said shaking the chain, "come to the side without holding on. It's one hand for the ship and one for yourself. No matter what you're working, it's always one for yourself. You ain't any help falling over the side."

"Yessir," the Kid said.

"What you doing out here?" Red asked.

"Watching. But I can't see it yet."

"See what?"

"The ocean. I've never seen water on all sides, or even on one side as far as I could see. At home we had mountains. I want to see it for myself. If you've only read about it or seen pictures, it's hard to believe."

"This is no tourist cruise. The Third Mate wants you in the wheel house. He said for me to find you and tell you. It's the highest room on the ship. You keep climbing ladders until you get there. Got it?"

"Yessir."

Red turned then turned back.

"It's not like I told you, Kid. You don't keep a hand on the railing because you might fall — it's because you might jump. Sometimes she will reach up and touch your face. When that happens, you hold on with *both* hands."

Red hopped onto the hatch, crossed a deck, and paused at the focsle door for a long breath to take inside. On the boat deck a light flicked on then off.

5

On the boat deck the Chief Cook flicked on the light for a quick look at his watch. He stretched the long length of himself in the sheets and touched his feet to the foot bar. The smell of soap hung in the room and brought a smile to his face. *Either soogee down the cook shack, deck to overhead, or get another cook* — in his ultimate voice to the Steward.

He stretched again. He'd almost played it too close this trip. But it was his way, his style. Something always came up. This time the S.S. *Ekonk*. Everything clean as a whistle, shipshape and first class, the only way to go. Except to the war zone. He had not ever again meant to go to a war zone. Two sinkings were enough. And God when that water-cooler strap gave at the blast and slapped him across the backside . . . at the memory he began to sweat.

Shouldn't lie here too long.

Not the first day.

They'd be two or three days getting the whiskey out of them. God what riffraff. And stink! Get the lemon and vanilla extracts out of the galley. Take the stuff to the Steward's room, dump it, and walk out. When they came threatening and shaking, he could honestly say, Steward took them. See him. Let the Steward fight them.

They won't be eating today, so put on a big show. A beef in aspic for a centerpiece — on a bed of patéd chicken livers. They'd remember seeing it. And really lay it on them for a week. Treat them every meal, then ride. One treat a week after that. The Steward was a belly robber, had the lowest grade of everything, but by God that didn't stop a real cook. Like everything else eating was ninety per cent show.

Fifteen more minutes, and he would get up and start his show. He knew how to do. How many other cooks brought them across washing decks to talk about bad-weather food? He sent them the daintiest sandwiches anybody could make. No crust and stuck with colored toothpicks he'd probably have to dye himself. Stewards.

He always waited in the closed-down galley. The big burly bastards came hand over hand on the lifelines to mince in the galley door waving a big dirty pinkie. "Hey,

Cookie, them girlie sandwiches, you trying to starve us? I had to eat thirty of them things to get a meal."

They loved it.

And the messboys would do what he said or everything they touched would be so hot and heavy they'd wish they were ordinary seamen. He'd go a few times himself to carve. Knock them right out of their skulls. He'd take the longest damned knife in the galley and carve each serving right before their eyes. Wave the knife and now and then carefully throw away a little piece or put it on top like a gem.

Give him two weeks. Not the Steward, not even the Captain could cross him.

He closed his eyes and half hummed half sang — *they threw the Chief Cook overboard and he's forty miles behind.*

Not this baby. He knew how to *do.*

You do right now and you look right, she said kneeling before him and straightening his suitcoat with a jerk hard enough to make him step for balance. *We are by ourselves now and living down here, but when we walk out that door we don't have to look it.*

And by God he never did. When he walked that street, he was different. He had to take a tire iron out with him one day and use it, but by God those dirty kids left him alone after that.

He flicked on the bunk light again. Ten minutes, *and he's forty miles behind.*

Three small taps sounded on the door.

"For Christ's sakes," the Cook said, "is somebody out there knocking?"

There was a long silence.

"Well?"

"*I* am."

"Well come in."

"Yessir."

The door eased back, and two blue eyes, one above the other, peeked through the crack.

"Excuse me, but I'm looking for the wheel house."

The Cook was on one elbow. "You got the wrong deck. You got to go forward then down then up again."

"Thank you."

The door started closing.

"Hey," the Cook cried. "Wait. What do you want the wheel house for?"

The door cracked again, and again two vertical blue eyes hung the space.

"The Third Mate wants me in the wheel house. You don't know what he wants, do you?"

"No, I don't know what he wants." The Cook threw back the sheet and reached for his pants. "But the thought that he wants you for what I think he wants you for just cost me ten minutes."

"What do you think he wants me for?"

"He wants to torture me. You can't find the wheel house, but you're going to steer the ship my stomach's first day at sea. He wants to zigzag me to death."

"Oh."

The door closed and the Kid turned back the way he came hoping he'd be able to find his way down. He didn't think that man or some of the others were very polite.

He found two down ladders, then one up. Passageways loomed dimly. Fireaxes hung the walls and black numbers were written on everything. He found more up ladders and walked through a rush of hot air into a room with a steel grating. The hot air through the grating ballooned his pants, and from far below the ship's engine pumped rhythmically. Suddenly he realized he had been feeling the engine ever since he woke up. When he'd opened his eyes he thought at first he was atop a loaded cotton wagon. But instead of his eyes meeting blue sky he stared at a white steel ceiling close enough to kiss.

He passed through a room with a long table and padded swivel chairs bolted to the floor. Everything was dark wood with a big sideboard on one wall covered with racks of shiny glasses in front of a long mirror. The mirrored sparkling glass dazzled his eyes, and behind them his face looked frightened. He went on and passed a door marked CAPTAIN. From behind the door came the tinkle of breaking glass. It was hard to know what to do here.

Then he climbed a ladder to a kind of walkway way up high and walked out to the end of it. He lifted his face to the night, and the engine throbbed and turned even up here. And up here it was like being on a big slow swing. Carefully he placed one hand on the railing.

"Hey, you out there."

He couldn't locate the voice at first. Then he saw the dim light in a cabin back up the walkway. He went to it. There was a man standing there behind a wheel.

"You signed on deck?" the man asked.

"Yessir. I'm an ordinary seaman."

"Well you're a helmsman now, Kid. Steering one seven five."

"One seven five?"

"That's right, and I'll be back in a damned minute."

The man disappeared into darkness, and he looked down

into the light at a circular card written with numbers and
letters and pictures. In the center a sea dragon waved its
tail and blew puffs of wind and waves. As he watched, the
number 175 went off to the right. He turned the wheel to
get it back, but it went past. So he turned it the other way,
and it went past again.

The more times the number passed the center mark the
faster it went and the longer it took to get it back.

He decided to wait and catch it as it came on around,
and 175 was just coming up from below with the dragon
puffing upside-down now and he thought sure he could
catch it and hold it where it was supposed to be, when the
man was standing there hollering at him.

He stepped off the grating, nodded, and told the man if
he didn't like the way he did it then he should do it himself.

"And stop damning me."

The Third Mate turned around three times and stopped
with his back to him.

There was a lot of confusion with somebody whistling
through a hole, and a voice in the hole asking what the hell
was going on. And the man running over to give the wheel
a spin and yelling into the hole that it was none of whoever
was in the hole's damned business. Then the man called
him over to the grating and said, "All right now. This," he
said rearing back and shaking himself against the spokes, "is
the wheel."

The man showed him how to do it, showed him how the
binnacle card always dipped before the card moved and
how the dip also told the direction it would go.

But he still couldn't do it.

He could only keep it between 115 and 196. The man
then had him steer by a star, but they all looked alike and

he couldn't keep track of which one he was supposed to be chasing, so they went back to the card.

Then he told the man he needed to go to the toilet.

"What?"

"The toilet," he said. "I got to go to the toilet."

"Toilet. Fifteen years. Toilet! Go on but don't leave the bridge. Go out there and piss over the damned edge. You go below and you'll damned well not find your way back. At least you can keep us going in the general direction. I *think* you're gaining on it."

The man took the wheel from him, and he started out to the end of the walkway.

"Damnit, not that way," the man shouted. "The wind's coming from that side you damned fool."

Hadn't met one with any manners yet.

6

In his cabin the Captain at his gray steel desk poured half Scotch, half water and no ice. He'd be the whole trip washing the shore from his mouth. The Port Captain had been a pompous ass, let you know every minute he was such a great captain he didn't have to do it anymore. That would never happen to him. He would never be a good enough captain to be something else.

And the Agent. "The company doesn't think you made good time last trip."

The company.

The *Agent* didn't think so. The owners with their names in the society headlines certainly didn't think he made a slow trip. They didn't even know him. The Agent said sign this, sign that, treated him like a deckhand. To the Agent it was all paperwork. The Agent had never been to sea!

As soon as they'd cleared the river to open sea, he told the Second Mate, "She's all yours, sir. Call me two days before we reach port, or if there is an emergency," and went directly to his cabin and stripped to his shorts. In the locker the cases were stacked one atop the other. He opened the first bottle of Black & White Scotch.

He drank and broke the first glass in the wastebasket. Soon the wastebasket was too deep with glass for breakage, and he began talking to himself, talking to the Agent, to the owners, to his wife. He had seen her only four days in the past year. Seventy-five per cent of every check went to the house she kept on the hill over the bay. The living room showed his travels, African teakwood, Japanese prints, ivory and jade figurines, crude spears and shields, knives from Indonesia, paintings made with the wings of South American butterflies, heads and skins of animals, and she watched over them like a museum.

He threw the glass against the far bulkhead.

At last it was happening. He was no longer talking to himself or to others. He was riding, sitting, swaying, feeling sleepy. Close his eyes, and he would be asleep, a dark dreamless sleep, and the Steward would hunt the dawn decks for the night's flying fish and serve them on a large platter. The ship lifted and slid deliciously on and on through what felt like a whole slow 360 degrees.

The 360-degree turn brought Gus's eyes staring open on a big round-headed rivet in the bulkhead, and he said, "Thirsty."

He felt under his pillow, but the hand came out empty.

"Goddamn," he said.

It was the first time in twenty-seven days there was nothing underneath the pillow, not since he paid off the coastal freighter and started this drunk. When it came to drinking he thought the second day better than the first, and the third better than the second, and then things started getting good. Each morning he pulled the bottle from beneath the pillow and before he got out of bed he was primed and ready.

Nobody rolled him and nobody stole his money over the counter unless he allowed it. He used no tricks. He put his money in the big seaman's wallet chained to his belt and walked. When he went ashore he rented a room and lived as "they" lived. He went to neighborhood bars, picked up women, and kept a bottle in his room. And he took care of himself as well as his money. He never missed a meal.

He had not apologized to a living thing about anything since the day he found out he wasn't *sorry* about anything.

If I was going to be sorry about it, I wouldn't have done it.

Saying sorry was only a way of getting somebody you had screwed to feel sorry for you. They had to hurt and like you too. And it was a lie anyway because he wasn't sorry.

And he never stepped back.

One night a man came through his door after a girl. "Come on," the man said. "Hand over the big purse."

"You come on," he said picking up a chair, "because if you don't I'm coming for you."

He beat the badger senseless, locked him in the closet, and fucked his woman one time right after another and made her whisper *I like it I like it I like it*. Anytime she stopped he put his hands around her throat. Then he locked her in with her badger and left.

Thirsty.

Rolling from the bottom bunk he went to the messroom in his shorts. He stepped over some guy on deck and searched through the refrigerator, then the room, the shelves, the cupboard, looked in all the used glasses. Nothing. He tried water, but it didn't help. He needed whiskey, big burning jolts of it to drive away the dry heavy pain.

His eyes caught two large bottles of hot pepper sauce on the table and wondered in amazement at the simplicity. With the hand bloody in a kitchen towel he unscrewed the bottle tops, dumped the contents into a pan, threw out the peppers, and drank. It burned good — seared his lips, thickened his tongue, and took all the air from his throat.

"Aaaaaaaaaaaaa," he said.

Before he got back to his bunk he turned back to the messroom. He drank some water, then he couldn't breathe. His throat wouldn't take air. He went back to the focsle and turned on the overhead light without hearing the grunts or stirs in the other bunks. He went back to the messroom for more water. He brought to the focsle a small table and brought more water and tea and ice and anything cold. Two cold bottles of catsup cooled his throat on either side. He brought platters of cold cuts, bread, milk — cold soothing milk around his tongue, but it wouldn't swallow. He couldn't get it down his throat.

Standing in the midst of the loaves and jars and bottles and platters with milk in his mouth, he reached into a bunk and gently shook someone's bare freckled shoulder. The man's head rolled on the pillow. Pointing urgently at his mouth, he shook the shoulder again.

Then he lay carefully down on the floor and with a low nasal moan passed out.

7

Only the back of the Kid's head stuck out of the binnacle when the Mate shook his arm for the second time. Again he shook off the Mate's hand. The needle was dead center and steady for the first time. If he looked up he would lose it, so he kept his head down and eased the wheel a spoke left.

"I said shove off," the Mate said. "Get some breakfast and turn in."

The Kid raised his head and found his back aching and the sun zooming over the horizon like today it would do the job in half the time.

The horizon.

Without a word the Kid walked stiffly from the wheel house onto the wing of the bridge. There she was. The circling horizon of water rose above him. He turned but couldn't see that part of her behind the wheel house, so he went back inside, saying "excuse me" to the Mate, and onto the other wing. Just like on the other side.

She saucered up everywhere, heavy, moving up and down like breathing, like she was resting. And far off on the horizon lay a smudge that somehow he knew was land, a continent of land as surrounded by water as the ship was. And again he was standing on the mountain with the seashells in his hand.

He had been digging sassafras roots when he found the spiraling shells. The next day the valley teacher told him they were seashells, that the ocean had left them on the mountain. For the rest of the day the clapboard walls would not hold his mind; it wondered the mountains.

At the last school bell he climbed Bald Mountain's side, not the winding road but straight up the mountainside at the branches of trees and brush growing straight up from the falling slope, sliding and kicking in his feet until at last there was only Bald Bluff, the living rock of the mountain, to pull himself onto. His feet stamped the backbone of the mountain that after he got over thinking his daddy was the strongest thing in the world he thought it was. He stood on the bluff in the glazing wind and saw it all happen. From a blue distance the water rose around him and over him. He flowed with the surging water over the land. He beat against the bluff until its rock was bare. He swept along, flashed down the valleys, pounded over the mountains, washed valleys deeper, crested the mountains. It took all his strength.

He stayed there until dark, knowing the whipping he would get would be worth it, and after the whipping was over he told them just as he had been telling them since half his life ago.

"Pshaw, boy," his father said incredulously. "You leaving home over a whipping? You've school to think of."

So he thought of school until he graduated, and that night after graduation, after the moon had gone down, he dropped the cardboard suitcase out his bedroom window. In the bare dirt yard he stopped beside the black iron washpot standing on three stones and looked out into the darkness. Somewhere off in the night a screech owl shrilled and down in the henhouse a rooster answered. He knelt there, one hand on the rim of the iron kettle. He could feel the land running under the night farther than his eyes had ever seen. On the iron rim his hand pulsed.

Standing on the wing of the bridge he slapped the railing. "Hot damn," he said. "I solid did it."

Painting the Ship

1

ON THE THIRD DAY at sea the land became a bad dream in the crew's memory. They woke up, and there was the ocean. They stood their watches and the ocean was around them, and when they went inside to sleep the ocean moved beneath them. Everyone started his routine, except the one who stank. He was called a "Black Satchel Man." The Bosun explained to the Kid that a Black Satchel Man never left the ship until he paid off. It took a suitcase to carry his money.

When the crew awoke the third day with most of their senses intact, there were some mutters about the odor. Gus still couldn't talk, so he grabbed Gene by the arm, pointed to Gene's mouth, then to the Satchel Man still thrown in his bunk.

". . . sun," the Satchel Man said, and Gene shook him again.

"You're not up there; I carried you down last night."

". . . uh?"

Before Gene carried him down, whoever happened to be on the focslehead rolled him out of the sun and Gus, licking swollen lips, twice took him some water, which he drank with closed eyes.

"Not the sun," Gene said. "A bath."

". . . tomorrow."

"Get up."

". . . tomorrow."

Gene turned to the circle of half-naked seamen. "Get a couple of buckets and a scrub brush."

That's when the Bosun crooked his finger at the Kid eating a ham and cheese and pickle and mustard and boiled tongue sandwich with mayonnaise and catsup. "Come on," he said.

The Kid and the Bosun bathed him. They didn't douse him on deck with buckets of water and use the scrub brushes. They laid him on the steel washroom deck and stripped him. The Kid slipped the Satchel Man's shorts while the Bosun held him by the armpits. The Satchel Man's penis was a tiny black peanut stuck in the gray hair. They propped him, sitting, in the back of a shower stall and adjusted the nozzle. The water showered the walls and splashed the slumping gray head.

"You can throw those over the side," the Bosun said, pointing to the shorts.

The Kid threw them out a porthole.

"Let him soak a while," the Bosun said.

They both washed their hands and came back in half an hour.

The Satchel Man was still black with spreading red tinges.

"Too hot," the Bosun said, adjusting the handles.

They stood him up holding the shower stall and soaped

him down. This time he came out red and white and black.
They soaped him down again and rinsed him again, and
the only black places were around his hands and face.

They walked him all white and red and exposed back to
the focsle, threw a sheet across his bunk, and dumped him
in.

"He'll start eating now," the Bosun said. "Be ready to go
tomorrow. Name is James. He is the best helmsman I've
ever known."

The Bosun crooked his finger again, and the Kid, munching
a piece of yellow cheese the size of his hand, took off behind
him like a heeling dog. Yesterday it was the paint locker,
but the Bosun wouldn't let him paint. They only talked
about painting. *You don't start at the bottom and paint
up,* the Bosun said in summation. *That's messboy stuff.*

Again they headed for the paint locker, and this time the
Bosun handed him a small bucket of paint and a brush.

"Really paint?" the Kid asked.

"Today," the Bosun said.

They started walking up and down ladders. The Kid
waited while the seventy-four-year-old, arthritic Bosun
climbed a step at a time, one-foot-up both-feet-on, one-foot-
up both-feet-on. At the top of one ladder the Bosun looked
back upon his success with a nod of approval, and one time,
rubbing his right knee, stopped halfway up a ladder, and
the Kid, looking up at the two worn white spots in the bag-
ging dungarees, wanted to put his shoulder to the fading
seat and help. But he didn't. Something in the Bosun's
face, his concentration on the leverages of arms and legs to
lower or raise his body, stopped the Kid from even the sim-
plest offer of a hand.

Stopping at the railing the Kid watched the white foam
float past and waited for the Bosun to get far ahead. Then

the Kid walked his own pace to catch up and skipped down
the ladder. The Bosun was at the foot pointing.

"There," the Bosun said.

"Where?"

"The mast."

Walking in among the winches the Kid looked at the
three-foot-thick mast rising from the deck and hanging with
straps and chains. He turned to the Bosun.

"With this little bitty bucketful?"

"You won't paint it all."

"Won't paint the first three feet."

"I told you — you are no messboy."

"What?"

"It's not the first three feet we're after," the Bosun said.

The Kid looked at the Bosun, then up. Except for the
mast the sky was an empty blue. Taut lines pushed up from
the ship's sides against the mast, and above them the crosstree thrust outward. It swung easily about in the blue, circling, and above it the remainder of the mast looked, he
thought, to be stirring the sky itself.

"Hey, Boats," the Kid said. "I know enough to know ordinary seamen don't work aloft. It's against the rules. Against
the law even."

"You got to learn it."

"Listen, I would be glad to do it for you, but I'm not supposed to. That's for when you become an A.B."

"You think one day they will hand you papers saying you
are now an able-bodied seaman and automatically your
head will fill up?"

"But it's against the law," the Kid said.

"Everything's against the law. You always have to do the
thing before they will let you."

"What?" the Kid said, shaking his head

"It's simple. Somebody teaches you."

"Maybe I don't want to be an A.B."

"Everybody wants to be an A.B.," the Bosun said. "They have to know about the ship they're on."

"Listen, Boats, I mean how much does what you want painted need it? Couldn't we wait and do it tomorrow or the next day or when we're in port? Look up there. She's rolling around a lot today."

The Bosun didn't look. "Calm as a kitten. Couldn't wish a better day."

The Kid put his hand on one of the rusting rungs, then took it quickly away.

"It's just to the crosstree," the Bosun said.

The Kid looked up, forty feet or more, and he knew from the mountains that down always looked three times farther than up did.

"Only the crosstree?"

"No more."

The Kid took hold of the rung again and set his foot on another. He found the bucket in his other hand and got down.

"Can't climb with this bucket, Boats. Sorry."

"I only filled it half full. Hook it in your elbow."

He knew enough not to look down. He looked at the pocked metal mast rusting inches before his eyes and climbed carefully.

"You're fine," the Bosun said. "Keep climbing."

At the crosstree he carefully eased one leg over the foot-and-a-half-wide beam, straddled it, and wrapped his arms around the mast. Even from up here the horizon of water rose above him. He floated slowly through the air on his giant centerless swing. Up and down, to the right and to the left, and forward and back in ever-changing circles through an empty sea and sky.

He heard the Bosun again. Looking down, he saw the Bosun as a face with arms and toes. ". . . the mast. How can you paint with your arms wrapping the mast?"

He unwrapped his arms and inched backward.

"Turn around," the Bosun called. "Turn around."

"And paint with my back to it?" The Kid's voice had anger in it

"Turn around. It's not the mast you're painting."

He maneuvered himself, holding a rung, and sat with both feet dangling forward. The ship eased down at the head. His legs swung out, and his stomach soared over his head. His seat floated off the metal beam. When he floated down again, he lifted his leg and was astraddle facing the other way. Ahead was an eight-foot length of beam narrowing to a six-inch width and emptiness.

"Out to the end," the Bosun said in his ear. "Get on your knees and go to the end. No. No," the voice said. "You can't hold it between your legs; you got to balance."

He was on his hands and knees amazed. The bucket, the brush sunk in paint, now dangled from his fingers gripping the diminishing beam. Ten inches, eight inches. Crawling on his hands and knees to the six-inch-wide end where he stopped with his head hanging over the end into nothing.

Nothing.

Now there was no way *not* to look down. There was nothing for the eye to hold to, only blue distance. Raising or lowering his eyes only changed the intensity of blue. He hung there in suspension. Then the ship lay down to the side, and he was sliding headfirst off the end into the blue void. His fingers squeezed into the metal's rusting pocks and pores.

"You're doing fine," the Bosun said in his ear. "Fine. Fine. You're all right now, you're all right. The thing I want you to do now: you take the bucket in one hand and the brush in the other, and you paint the thing you're standing on, the underside of it."

"Underside?"

"Underside."

He began the deliberate process of changing the bucket from one set of gripping fingers to the other. For one brief moment both hands were in the air, and he was balanced in space on his knees.

"You're all right," the Bosun said. "I don't mind if paint drips. That is the way. You don't need both hands. Now lean out. That's it. Now paint the underside."

He leaned into the blue, and he and the beam turned upside-down. He hung by his knees and he and the beam circled together in the gentle uneven circles of sea and sky — he holding the beam on his knees and painting its other side with a protective coat of red lead.

As he redipped the brush in the circling upside-down bucket, the Bosun said in his ear, "That's enough. Back up now, don't try to turn around. Back up."

He backed his feet against the mast, then he straddled the beam and looked down into the Bosun's face. Their eyes touched over the distance. They were both grinning from ear to ear. And he saw on an upper deck the Chief Mate standing and watching. The sun shone on the Mate's naked body reflecting the tattoos in feathery iridescences. The Mate disappeared into a companionway.

Back on deck, the Kid stamped his feet. "God!" he said.

"We'll clean the brush now," the Bosun said.

He fairly skipped ahead at times, and the Bosun hurried to keep up. The Bosun shuffled hard and slid his feet six inches at a time, and whenever the Bosun passed a hatchway he went, "Toot, toot," as a warning not to step out and knock him flying. "Toot, toot," sliding his six-inch steps. "Toot, toot," at the bent backside of an A.B. flaking line on the deck.

At the head of a ladder the Kid, waiting for the Bosun to pull himself up, suddenly reached back for the Bosun's hand and gave it a hearty pull.

"Well," the Bosun said. "Well, how about that."

2

"Toot, toot," the Kid said at the door of the messroom.

Gene, bare above the round brass buckle at his waist and with a black watch cap back on his blond head, stood in the center of the messroom mixing an Aqua Velva-after-shave-lotion-cocktail. Sailors were gathering half-naked, pulling off gloves or wiping sleep from their eyes, to look at the blue-green bottle of Aqua Velva atop a napkin holder in the center of the table, four ounces and nearly full.

"Look at us," a squat A.B. against the wall said. "We're standing on a million bottles of beer looking at four ounces of shave lotion. I was in the table over that beer hold today and saw a hatch with one loose dog between us and it."

"One loose dog's enough," Gene said. "The dog's got to be off. Look." Gene held out a tray of ice cubes for all to see. Dumping the ice in a dishtowel, he snowed that around, then a ball-peen hammer, which brought a stir and mum-

bling. He crushed the bag of ice with the hammer, tested
its coarseness, and beat it some more. He lined up his con-
diments and tools: limes, sugar, a spoon, a quart fruit jar
with a lid, a strainer. He stuck a water glass into the mound
of crushed ice, squeezed the limes into a jar, added sugar,
fingered a taste to the tip of his tongue, and gave a satisfied
smack.

He showed around the Aqua Velva like a picture in his
palm.

"Gentlemen," he said and unscrewed the cap. He measured half into the jar. Then raising his hands in a gesture
of resignation and abandonment, he dumped in the rest.

"AAAAAAAh," someone said.

All eyes followed the jar as Gene shook it violently and
professionally until it frosted. Before unscrewing the lid,
he rubbed his cold hands on the pale transparent skin of his
stomach and closed his eyes.

Then he led them out to the number one hatch with the
brimming cold glass. Some sat on deck, some on the hatch,
some stood at the railing.

After settling himself on the hatch Gene raised the glass
to them. He nibbled the cold rim and raised his eyes heav-
enward. A smile spread his lips.

"That's the wrong kind." Gus at the railing mumbled his
first words since drinking the pepper sauce.

Gene's eyes never raised. "Wrong kind of pepper
sauce?"

"Alcohol."

"Listen to the pepper sauce konisewer."

"It'll blind you," Gus said, not moving his pink, peeling,
swollen lips.

Gene's muscles quickened with laughter beneath the pale,

blue-veined skin. He slowly drank half the glass and blew his lung-warmed air through pursed lips. "Blind *me*? It wouldn't dare."

"Ha!" Gus's mouth opened wide in spite of himself.

"You think I couldn't do blind?" Gene asked. "You think being blind would curl me up. I know a blind man. I could be a blind man. Easy."

Gene slipped off the hatch and stood with the watch cap pushed back and clogs on his feet. "Who would like some?"

He held out the glass, turning and qustioning.

"Anybody? Anybody else think you could do blind?"

"I could."

A short man with silky black hair over his chest and shoulders and arms said, "Shit, I can be anything," and reached for the glass, but his hand closed on air.

"You can't be it on my stuff, Blackie. Get your own," Gene said, sitting back on the hatch. He sipped at the glass, measured, and sipped again. "Here Mister Anything," he said, handing over the last quarter inch to Blackie. "Taste what it's like."

The Bosun watching from the hatchway leading into the focsle said, "No." He turned to the Kid, "Come on, we will get some coffee." As they passed the messboys' foscle, they heard a mumble of curses in the shadows.

In the shadows of the focsle the tiny messboy called Peewee cursed monotonously because the Steward had switched him from the officers' mess to the crew's mess and because that morning the syph had come back on him.

Peewee was exactly five feet and two inches tall. He had a short blond mustache and a cocky walk, and he had come awake knowing the syph was back. His hand under the sheet reached down and touched the chancre, and he started cursing. Switching on his guarded bunk light he looked at it. The new chancre was the final link in the circling chain of old scars. He dressed and went to see the Captain. It was several minutes before he could get the Captain to the door, and when the door opened he didn't wait for an invitation he pushed the startled Captain aside and walked in.

He saw without noticing the wastebasket full of glass and glasses, and vaguely he was aware of deeply inhaling the fumes of Scotch. He walked over to the tumbled covers on the Captain's bunk, back to the door, back to the bunk again.

The Captain, in his pajama bottoms and rubbing the back of his neck and swaying with dizziness, watched him race up and down the cabin and wondered if he still couldn't be asleep and dreaming. If the Captain was expecting anybody, which he wasn't, it was the Steward with a plate of flying fish. The Captain stumbled around the wastebasket and eased into the padded swivel chair before the blue-green desk cleared except for two half-empty bottles of Scotch and a quart jar of red vitamin pills. The Captain saw Peewee's mouth going and began to hear him.

"Three times they told me I was cured and back it comes. I get out of the hospital and *boom* I'm back again. Other times I was sailing coastwise; this time I'm foreign and look."

Peewee stopped pacing, and the Captain, at most expecting a plate of flying fish, found Peewee's penis waving six inches in front of his face.

"Hey, put that thing up," he said.

"Look at it," Peewee said.

The Captain would have risen if it hadn't meant leaning forward.

"I don't know what your problem is, Sailor, but whatever it is you take it out of my cabin." The Captain sat stiffly erect holding the chair arms and his head back.

Peewee looked at him sitting there all stiffed up and suddenly his mouth opened and he stepped back indignantly.

"Here now," Peewee said outraged. "It's not anything like that. Just because I'm a messboy you can't . . . Look," Peewee said coming back and turning it over so the Captain could see the chancre. "The syph is back on me."

With unsteady hands the Captain settled a pair of glasses on the end of his nose and looked.

"I should say you have," he pronounced. "The syph has come back on you. Turn it over the other way. Huuuuu . . . Now the other way. Huuuuuuu . . . I've got some good news for you, Sailor. That last chancre has completely circumsized you. How about that?"

"Shit," Peewee said.

"How are you signed on?" the Captain asked.

"Messman. Officers' messman."

"Oh? Well, we can't have that. I'll have a talk with the Steward about that. Now let me see what we have in the medicine chest."

The Captain fumbled a key from the desk and opened a locker. "Mostly things for pain. How long did you say you've had this?"

"Three years."

"Well now I see no emergency here then, do you? I mean after three years I could hardly call the coast guard to come running."

"I guess not," Peewee said. "But . . ."

"Or put into port on an emergency basis. Here now let me look this up in the book."

The Captain thumbed a thick book he took from the locker, and Peewee said, "It may not be *that* kind of emergency but . . ."

"I'm reading, Sailor."

The Captain read along over the top of his finger saying, "Uuuuum. Uuuum. No. No. No, not much we can do there. No. Uuuuuum."

He put the book back and began looking around the locker, picking up different jars and bottles, moving them around and shaking them. "Here we are," he said, giving a package a good shake. "Just the thing."

He handed over the package and Peewee said, "What is it?"

"Soap," the Captain said. "*Medicated* soap. Here, take two more bars. Now, what I want you to do, what I insist that you do, is wash yourself before every meal. Each time you go on duty you are to wash yourself. Is that understood?"

"Yessir, but . . ."

"No buts. I understand the Steward's department is one man short already. Can't take you off duty, you *have* to remember to wash."

"But . . ."

"No buts! You wash yourself or I'll have your papers. What's your name?"

"I'm called Peewee."

"That's funny," the Captain said. "Peewee." With a hand on Peewee's shoulder he led him to the door. "One thing. If you run out of soap, you see me for more. Right?"

"Right," Peewee said.

He stuck the bars of soap in his pocket so no one would

ask questions and went back to the focsle. He waited until the other messmen left before he took a round can the tobacco companies vacuum-pack for seamen, fifty cigarettes at a time, and half filled the can with warm water. In his shadowy top bunk with the can between his legs he washed his chancre with medicated soap. He had washed his chancre before serving breakfast; he washed it before serving lunch, after which the Steward told him he was the crew's messman now, not the officers'.

Now he was sitting in his bunk, cursing, with the cigarette tin between his legs, carefully soaking his chancre in medicated soap in preparation for serving supper.

In the 115-degree heat of the engine room Slim the Oiler made his rounds with pent-up sweat pouring from his white pores. After supper he would head straight for his bunk. He could hardly wait. Sleep like a baby tonight. Already he was getting back into the swing of it. He climbed and slid down ladders connecting the tiers of walkways over and around the great reciprocating engine. Tied to the walkways at various places were all shapes and sizes of oil cans and oil buckets with paintbrushes in them.

He slid down the railings of a ten-foot ladder as gracefully as a bird dropping from a branch. He let the forces of the slide carry him to the bucket of oil tied exactly to the spot his hand passed to reach the piston driving in and out of its sleeve. Already he was in sync with the piston's motion; he'd synced in coming down the ladder. Slip slap slap, he hit the briefly exposed cylinder three times with the brush and was off again. He never turned the wrong way or wasted one step. He tossed himself up the ladders, and in weather he let the heaving of the ship move him over and around the engine, as he squirted and slapped oil into moving cups and holes and joints.

At the end of his round, he slid down a ladder and eased to a stop beside the Fat Fireman beneath a ventilator. The ventilator ran up through the ship to the boat deck where its wide mouth opened to the wind. Under the ventilator the temperature was a cool ninety. Slim the Oiler swiped his forehead with a rag hanging from a back pocket, and the Fat Fireman nodded in sympathy.

Slim cocked a critical ear to the heaving, sibilant engine. He didn't want any trace of pounding. The First Engineer told each of the three oilers, "*Six quarts a watch. That's it.*" He'd show the stingy bastard. He'd oil her with four, stash the extra two in a good place until he had his own emergency supply, then for the rest of the trip he'd oil her with four and dump the extra two in the bilges. And she wouldn't pound a lick. Not on his watch.

The Fat Fireman nodded again and walked away to check his boilers. He checked the needles on his gauges. He stopped to tap one and wiped his hands on the rag. Satisfied, he settled himself on a stool beneath another ventilator. Both he and the Oiler had decided to sail in the blackgang because they wanted to learn a trade for when they quit going to sea. Both still talked of the possibility and knew the latest hourly shore wage for their skills.

The Second Engineer stood beneath another ventilator. The handles on his telegraph stood at full ahead. Before his face was the speaking tube to the bridge and beneath his hand, the ship's throttle, the wheel he turned to regulate the engine's revolutions. The Second, too, had chosen the engine room to learn a trade, but unlike Slim and the Fireman he learned long ago that he would never quit the ships.

When the watch was over and the three of them went topside, Slim took a long leisurely shower. The sweat had taken out all the poisons, as he liked to say, and now he washed them down the drain to the sea. The water sparkled in his light hair and down the long muscles of his white body. He didn't like the sun, never took sunbaths because it stopped up the pores. Drying himself he slipped on the faded soft blue shirt and dungarees that he had washed the watch before and dried in the fiddley, and he turned off the steam line bubbling water in the bucket of clothes from his last watch.

He was clean and his stomach was light and all his poisons washed away. He floated into the messroom. The tables were covered with white cloths, and on the sideboards were bowls of green onions and olives and pickles and salads. Peewee came in straining under the weight of a steam bucket in either hand.

"I heard you were ours now," Slim said.

"Lucky you," Peewee said, fitting the buckets into the steam table and going back out the door.

The Fat Fireman was already sitting with some others at one of the tables waiting for supper. "What are we going to do about this?" the Fat Fireman said.

"We can't do *nothing*," one of the others said.

"We got to call a meeting."

"Yeah," a deckhand said.

The Fat Fireman stuck his head out the door and hollered "Union meeting" into the focsle and in they came shuffling and muttering, knowing already what it was all about.

"I don't mind his syph," Gene said, still disappointed because the Aqua Velva hadn't done much for him. "It's not so much the syph it's sending him to us when they find he's got it that gets me."

"That's it."

"Anything dirty, give it to the crew."

"They couldn't take syph."

"I was on this ship," Blackie said, stroking the silky hair on the back of his hand. "Had bedbugs. We started throwing mattresses over the side and got action fast."

"You mean we ought to throw Peewee overboard?" someone asked.

"Yeah."

" 'At's it."

"Deep-six him."

They began laughing and clapping.

Then the Cook came bending through the doorway. He was all in white, shoes, pants, apron, shirt, and a chef's cap standing a crisp white foot above his head. He carried a spiked hone in one hand and a long whippy carving knife in the other. Behind him came Peewee leaning under the weight of two great glistening roasts on a scrubbed two-foot-wide plank.

"Godamighty, somebody help me," Peewee gasped.

With his white hat almost touching the overhead, the Cook directed the placing of the meat while slipping the blade on the hone. "Gentlemen, help yourself to that stack of warmed dinner plates Peewee's prepared and line along here for your preference."

The Fat Fireman was first in line.

"What'll it be? The rare one on the left? Well done or some of both? Rare? Maybe just a taste of outside?"

Brown and red juices oozed down the side of the two-foot-high roasts. The Cook covered their plates with two-inch-thick slices, sometimes reaching out with his knife to cut away some tiny offending piece only he could recognize.

"There," he said. "Wait, wait, you must try this little piece of outside." He topped the heavy slice with a dark sliver. Peewee surrounded the slabs of bleeding beef with smoking mashed potatoes and moved up and down the tables offering bowls of tiny green onions and black and green olives and sweating rolls and pestering them to ask for anything else.

The Fat Fireman ate happily and continuously. He swallowed half-chewed meat and pushed in more, breathing heavily, head down. He bit and chewed and swallowed all at the same time. Across from him, beside the Bosun, the Satchel Man watched and was sick. The Satchel Man tried the meat but it made his teeth hurt. The Bosun's elbow urged his arm, and he tongued a fork of mashed potatoes to the roof of his mouth and sucked. Then he tried some peas on the fork, but they shook off. He tried again, gave up, and switched to a spoon. He mashed the peas with his tongue as the Bosun nudged him again.

"I am, Boats. I am." He looked at the Fireman and grimaced.

The Cook wiped and honed his blade, and the Fat Fireman, shoving all the way, led them back for more. Peewee, filling coffee cups, insisted there was something else he could do.

Soon they were waving away the potatoes and peas. Some rested. Some began to talk.

"Great grub."

"Man."

"I'm stuffed."

Peewee pestered them to take more. "A green onion. How about you? You Gene? Gus, how about a taste more meat? A taste of outside?"

"Well . . ."

"Just a taste of outside for Gus, Cook," Peewee said handing over the plate. "And a little of the rare just in case."

A deckhand leaned back and put both hands on his stomach. "Cook, you really know your galley."

The Cook lifted his knife to him.

"New fresh coffee. Anybody for new fresh coffee?" Peewee asked.

The Fat Fireman was back for one last slab of meat as the others were beginning to leave. "Cookie," the Fat Fireman said chewing out the words, "that was a great piece of meat."

They stretched their stomachs and groaned as they left, most of them carrying coffee cups.

"Thanks, Cookie."

". . . best meal I ever had aboard ship."

"The best *cook* I ever had."

"Great grub, Cook."

"Good."

"Fresh coffee anyone? It's new."

"Good meal, Cookie."

"That was chow."

"Delicious."

"Thanks, Cookie. Thanks."

The Cook's face was flushed with pleasure. "Thank *you*," he said, waving his knife. "Thank you *all*."

They gathered around the number one hatch, some holding coffee cups, some lying back on the hatch holding their stomachs. The Fat Fireman came up pushing his belt farther under his stomach. He backed up shoving himself onto the hatch and said into the silence, "Now what are we going to do about Peewee's syph. We can't let the officers put him on us because they can't do syph."

Gene sat upright with a groan. "For all I care right now Peewee can bottle his syph and use it for seasoning." With another groan he lay back down.

"Yeah."

"Who cares."

"What do you think, Boats?"

The Bosun was at the railing with the pale and shaky Black Satchel Man. "He is aboard. He has to be somewhere."

The Bosun walked to the other end of the well deck, turned, and when he came back turned again. The Black Satchel Man came off the railing and wordlessly walked with him. They went slowly back and forth the length of the well deck in an even pace, the Bosun sliding his feet and the Satchel Man, not yet with his sea legs, weaving at the Bosun's shoulder. They soon stopped, but two other older ones took it up, an A.B. with wild gray hair and a shriveled electrician. Soon Red hopped off the hatch and joined them. The three of them silently paced the deck, not walking in step, but the space between their shoulders never varied as they went straight down the deck to turn in unison and come straight back. The Kid, his stomach aching so he could hardly breathe, looked at them and wondered if he could ever do it. When he walked, he went all over the deck.

The day was almost over. They watched the sun settle into the sea and the waves come in. They stood along the railing, or sat on the hatches, or walked and watched the waters. The waves quartered in fresh off the bow and tugged ancient memories.

Red's shout broke the silence. "Look!" He was at the railing hopping and pointing.

They crowded the railing. Beyond the long blue swells

ahead the horizon boiled and flashed with blackness moving
toward them. They ran for the ladders to the focslehead,
and by the time they reached it the sea boiled only half as
far away.

"Mate," they shouted to the bridge. "Mate, dead ahead
and closing."

The Mate came on the bridge wing, looked, and ran back
inside the wheel house. He came back raising binoculars.
The Wheel Watch left the wheel and stood beside the
Mate. The Mate handed him the glasses and ducked back
inside. The Wheel Watch moved the glasses slowly back
and forth. His voice was amazed. "It's fish," he shouted
down. "A whole ocean of fish."

From horizon to horizon the ocean was black with leaping fish closing at speed.

"They're porpoises," Gus whispered.

"Godamighty, look at 'em jump," Peewee said in awe.

"I've never seen this."

". . . not in thirty years."

The heavy-bodied porpoises swam around the ship leaping and diving over each other. The ship sailed on porpoises.

"You could walk to the horizon," Gus marveled.

"Ain't ever even *heard* of it."

"Hey, Boats, you ever seen this?" Gene asked.

"I have never seen it," the Bosun said without turning.

"They ought to be stories about this, but who's heard
'em."

"Think I have," the Satchel Man said. "Something about
a migration, or maybe seeing them I only think I heard."

Men came up from the engine room to see the leaping
mass of life. The Chief Mate came out of his room to stand

naked in his tattoos, both hands on the railing. Only the
Captain drunk in his bunk in a dreamless sleep had to be
told.

When the sun disappeared and darkness covered the
ocean, the men began to leave the decks and go to their
bunks. They pulled shut makeshift curtains, wedged pillows
about their shoulders. Some lit bunk lights and read themselves drowsy while others rocked in the darkness and
dreamed themselves to sleep.

The Kid, when the dark came, stood his watch on the focslehead as lookout. From the bow he watched an ocean
alive. He could no longer see the bodies leaping in the
darkness, only their trails. They dragged long trails of flashing phosphorus through ghostly leaps and dives. The
ocean sparked with arcs of golden phosphorus. Beneath
the black sky, light reversed itself and came from the
depths.

The porpoises were gone long before the Kid's watch was
over. He paced the focslehead alone, and later in his bunk
he dreamed of a great teeming herd of porpoises swimming
over Bald Bluff and leaping down the valley toward his
home.

3

Each day after supper they sat on the hatch and watched
the waves come in and the day end. They talked or walked
the decks in unison. The Kid for the first time in his life
found his pockets empty. When he changed his khakis he
had nothing in his pockets to transfer. Once a week the
Steward opened the slopchest, and they signed for toiletries,

cigarettes, needles and thread, work clothes. There were no newspapers. The shriveled electrician had a radio, but he seldom listened to it. Sparks spread the news, the big news. Sparks heard it in his radio shack and passed it on at the mess. They read the weather: the wind, the sky, and the water. And as the ship traveled through different currents and latitudes their dress changed with the temperatures.

Except for the few day men like the Bosun or the Steward's department, they worked four hours on and eight hours off. A solid eight hours' sleep became a thing of the past. One off-watch was for the major sleep, the other for a nap. And only one of the three watches ate all the regular meals in the messroom. Another ate lunch as breakfast, and another tended to miss lunch.

They read.

Their library was a large foot locker of books. They read whatever they found in the locker and believed what they read. Those with good memories had heads stuffed with masses of stories and information and words they couldn't pronounce.

They changed their linens twice a week and washed and mended their clothes. The Satchel Man had the neatest stitches aboard. He snagged his new khakis on a cable and patched them with precisely slanted stiches. They soaked their clothes in buckets of water bubbling with live steam.

One afternoon the Kid and the Bosun were chipping paint when the Mate leaned down over the bridge railing. "Whales," he called pointing.

They went to the railing. Five whales were blowing about a mile to starboard. "Hey," the Kid called to the Chief Mate sunning naked in a deck chair. "Look at the whales." The Cook and Steward looked up from peeling potatoes beneath a canvas awning outside the galley. Peewee came out of the galley with a load of bread, and when he got back to the messroom he hollered into the focsle. "Hey! Warta see some whales?"

They gathered on deck. As they watched, a sixth whale grew slowly from the water beneath a white plume.

And they passed a land mass.

Far off on the horizon it lay green and black beneath a bank of heavy clouds. They saw only the mountains and not the body of land below the water.

And one day they passed between two tiny uninhabited islands. The sea was a deep pure blue and the islands bright green with a fringe of brown rock. A necklace of white foam sparkled around the rocks. The ship passed between the islands, and the Kid could have thrown a rock onto the grass of either. In the center of each island swayed a cluster of palms, and looking across the grass and through the palms to the white foam beyond, the Kid felt he was looking upon a place no man had ever touched, and knew he would remember.

As he lay in his bunk that night he saw in the darkness the islands as they would always be in his mind, the purest place he had ever seen. Bald Bluff had never been like this. Standing on the mountain in the glazing wind he was always conscious of others standing beside him, of naked Indians with stones in their hands, buckskinned trappers, bearded men with rifles, men on horseback. Ghostly men crowded around him to look out over the river and valley and over the distant blue mountains. They brushed his arms and stepped in mocassins and boots to the edge of rock where the world quit and the stomach and head thrilled to emptiness.

At exactly three-twenty in the morning he heard the Watch come through the focsle door to wake him and was awake. He dressed in darkness and went in cool darkness to the messroom and the odor of fresh coffee. Sipping coffee, he breathed the bread heating in the toaster. The odor of toast warmed the room, and Gene came in pulling on a shirt and sat down. The Kid handed him a cup of coffee. The Fat Fireman came in and pulled the platter of cold cuts from the refrigerator and began eating. Slim the Oiler passed the door, waved, and left without a word.

The Kid and Gene crossed the dark decks through a cool breeze. At a down ladder the Kid said, "See you."

"Yeah," Gene said.

As the Kid climbed the last ladder to the focslehead, he saw in the dimness Red reaching for the focslehead bell and at the same time heard from the bridge the dong-dong dong-dong dong-dong dong-dong of the eight bells closing the watch. Red rang eight bells back to the bridge and cupped his mouth.

"Lights are *bright*, sir!"

A faint *thank you* drifted as over water back from the bridge.

In the darkness the Kid leaned into the v of the bow feeling the wind on his right cheek. Red came beside him and spoke in a quiet voice.

"Lots of lights tonight."

"Okay."

"Shipping lane."

"I'll watch out."

"Mate says about this time tomorrow we'll be in the war zone."

"That's what the Bosun told me," the Kid said. "He said it's the same as any other place."

"They move it around," Red said. "Sometimes it's here, sometimes there, and sometimes it's any ocean you're on. They always keep it going somewhere. It's the ones we get to run things."

"That's what the Bosun said. He said never put two bosses in the same room. You know he's a German?" the Kid asked.

"Lot of krautheads around, make good sailors."

"No, I mean a citizen. He's a German citizen. He sails our ships and he was sunk back in World War Two by Germans."

"That a fact. You know what the Skipper is?" Red asked.

"No."

"He's a Bluenose."

"What is that?"

"Nova Scotian. Lots of Bluenose officers, always on deck though. Never met a Bluenose engineer. You know what the tattooed Mate is?"

"No."

"Neither do I," Red said, "but whatever he is, he's tough. He came out of that chair the other day to where I was painting. Called me a slow sonofabitch. I'd of slapped him with the paintbrush had there been a spot left open. Colorful bastard. You know he's got a rabbit diving through grass up his asshole, only the rabbit's furry feet and tail are sticking out."

"Bosun told me they say that about all picture galleries."

"No really. His nickname's Stormy, but don't ever call him that. He got the name and them knobby legs in a typhoon. He was trying to cut loose an anchor and a wave blew him all the way over the bridge. Broke both legs with the bones sticking out. He locked his door and set them himself."

"They look it," the Kid said.

"I guess so. Oh, and me! You know what I am?"

"No."

"Guess," Red said.

"I don't know."

"Come on guess. I almost forgot me."

"I don't know."

"Try."

The Kid looked at his red hair. "Irish?"

"Wrong. I can show you on my seaman's papers. Says, address, Seamen's Institute, South Street, New York City. But it says, born, Saint Petersburg, Russia. Bet you didn't know I was Russian, did you, Kid?"

"Sure didn't."

Red scratched the back of his neck. "Don't even know the lingo. Fact is I read Saint Petersburg isn't Saint Petersburg anymore. Where you from, Kid?"

"Arkansas. The mountain side."

"Lot of farmers go to sea," Red said. "You know there's a whole farm county in Virginia that goes to sea. They say there's nothing up there but women and that when one of the sailors comes home he does the best he can but faced with a whole county there isn't much he can do. I was thinking of going up there next trip. Have a look-see."

"If you've got your mind on it, maybe you ought to do it," the Kid said.

"May just," Red said. "I see you got a light coming up there off the bow."

"I see it."

"Well she's all yours."

"I got it."

Red lifted his arms to the dark. "Beautiful night. Am I ever going to sleep!"

"Good night, Red."

"Night, Kid."

The Kid rang two bells to the bridge. "Point off the port *bow*," he called.

Thank you drifted from the dark bridge.

He stood in the v of the bow listening to the ship cut the water. It *was* a beautiful night but not a lucky night. Lucky nights porpoises kept him company. They played with the bow, trailing phosphorus and leaping and tumbling like children. They went wherever the ship went.

He watched the ship closing portside, a big one. The crew of the tanker they passed last week leaned on the railing to watch them and they watched back. Fifty yards away and no one spoke. Each crew watched a crew of men isolated on a ship at sea. Someone on the tanker without raising an arm from the railing lifted a hand. The Bosun lifted his hand, and he lifted his. Then everyone did it. As the fantails passed the crews looked after each other.

Dong. The one bell from the bridge startled him, and he scrambled around the anchor winch checking the running lights, the red, the green, two whites. He slapped the clapper one time against the focsle bell. "Lights are *bright*, sir."

Thank you.

With lights burning all over her the big ship neared on the portside. She came riding high, lighting the ocean. On the wing of the *Ekonk's* bridge the Mate watched the liner.

People partied on the liner. Colored lanterns strung her foredeck. People danced, and the *Ekonk* rode into a swirl of lights and music and muffle of voices. Some of them saw the *Ekonk* and waved and shouted against the lights. Others came to the railings carrying glasses. They beckoned and shouted faintly.

"Hi down there."

"Join the party."

The Kid lifted his hand, but the Mate watched silently.

After she had passed the Kid tried to imagine standing watch on her while the sun began and ended each day. He couldn't and so quit thinking about it.

As he was leaving the focslehead after sunrise, a brown rock rose ahead, and he rang it to the bridge, an abrupt rectangle of bare granite, ten feet high and perfectly flat on top. It sat the size of a large room, its sides straight and smooth. On the rock surrounded by ocean stood a huge seabird. Its dark eyes watched him as he passed.

War Zone

1

THE KID had been ringing bells and calling lights ever since he got on the focslehead. Lights strung the ocean like a circus midway. The *Ekonk*'s engine slowed to steerage, and when the sun came up she rode in a carnival of ships. Little ships, big ships, ships flying flags he had never seen, ships with well decks, poop decks, flush decks, ships all painted black except the sleek, leaden-gray sheep-dog ships racing among the Plimsoll-lined merchantmen. The sheep dogs mounted guns, and their decks and superstructure were clotted with blue-clothed men.

From the edge of his bunk last night, just before he pulled the makeshift curtain, he had said, "Boats, how will we know when we're in the war zone?"

"There are no markers, no buoys," the Bosun said. "They have charts and instruments. They measure the sun and stars to find it."

The Bosun had gone into the washroom. He swung his legs into the bunk and was pulling the curtain when Red came with a towel over his shoulders. "Hee-hee. Don't you worry, Kid. You and me won't need charts to know."

From the focslehead the Kid looked at the ships around him, and he looked to the bridge to see if the Mate was watching him leave the focslehead. The Mate waved acknowledgment. Above the sound of the *Ekonk*'s slowed engine, airplanes whined and roared from the thick bank of stratus clouds low overhead. Occasionally there was a long popping string of giant firecrackers.

The sun was a cloudy half and half on the horizon, and he was halfway down the focslehead ladder when the bank of cloud exploded in light. He looked up from the ladder waiting for the thunder to follow, and seconds later it did, an explosion curiously unequal to the light. On the port wing of the bridge, the Captain stepped out and peered upward beneath his gold-braided cap. He crossed two decks. The Bosun, coffee cup in hand, stepped out a hatchway looking upward, and he went to him saying, "Hey, Boats, we're in the war zone now," when a hunk of metal the size of two hands thudded onto the deck, bounced once, and lay dark and smoking between their feet.

Coffee sloshed from the Bosun's cup. "Gott."

The Bosun backed into the hatchway, and the Kid looked up into a splash of rain on his chin. Bits of metal bounced on the deck, rang among the winches, and ricocheted from the housing. The ocean splashed with white, and a dark heaviness fell to port. Bells and horns clanged and honked from the ships. Suddenly covering the top of his head with his arms the Kid dove into the hatchway beside the Bosun.

Others crowded from the messroom and the focsles.

"What the hell happened?" Blackie asked.

"What is it?"

"It was the cloud," the Kid said. "Like lightning."

"What?"

"Kid said the cloud exploded."

"Fucking clouds don't explode. What happened?"

"Look at those decks."

"The housing."

The white housing was splotched with red droplets. Even as they watched more appeared.

Gus pushed his way through.

"What is it?"

"Look at the housing."

"Look at the Kid," Gus said.

"Where?" the Kid said.

"What is it?" the Bosun said turning to the Kid. "You got hit?" He lifted the Kid's face between his palms.

"Hey, what are you doing?" the Kid said.

Gus stuck a thick hand between the Bosun's and wiped a thumb across the Kid's chin. "He's not hit," Gus said.

"It's blood," the Bosun said.

They looked at the splotched housing.

"Do," Gus said and started through the hatchway. The Kid and Bosun grabbed his thick arms, and he dragged them out with him before he broke loose and lurched to a halt on deck. For the first time Gus saw the metal. He looked vaguely around. "Do," he said again. Then his head jerked up. He leaped aside as something thudded to the deck beside him. He leaned over it. Then he looked at the cloud and back again. He circled the object on deck, looking from all sides. He circled once all the way around, then twice, before dropping to his knees for a closer look.

"Come back," the Bosun called.

Gus turned his head and looked at them with blank eyes.

"Take cover, Gus."

"Come back here," the Bosun ordered.

His blank eyes went back to the deck. A piece of metal clanged on the ladder and bounced over the side. He didn't move.

"*On deck there,*" cried an amplified voice.

The Captain stood on the exposed wing of the bridge with a bullhorn to his face.

"*I have sounded general quarters. I have sounded general quarters there.*"

Gus looked at them with round eyes.

"Come on, Gus," the Kid pleaded.

Gus cupped the thing in his hands and rose from his knees. With outstretched arms he came down the deck and into the companionway.

"What is that?" the Kid asked.

In Gus's hands it was black and red and pink, and Gus's hands were red.

"That's not metal."

"What is that?" the Kid asked. "Tell me what that is."

"It's meat."

The flesh plopped wetly on deck. Gus rushed at them holding out bloody hands. They gave as before a plow. Gus went into the washroom. A shower started.

It was about six inches long and nearly as wide, red and black and pink.

"Please tell me what that is?"

"*General quarters,*" the bullhorn said as another piece of metal clanged on the outside deck.

Gus came out of the washroom and pushed his way back through. Water ran down his clothes and legs and off his shoes onto the deck and against the black flesh.

"Hey, Gus," the Satchel Man said. "You didn't take your clothes off."

"I got to know," the Kid said.

The Bosun knelt with cumbersome care and with a key turned the dark flesh. A slick round of bone, white as milk, oozed from one end.

"I think it's a piece of somebody's arm," the Bosun said to the Kid. "It looks like arm. Peewee, get something to put this in."

"What's the black?"

"Might be burnt or off a black arm, or both," the Bosun said.

Peewee came with a two-pronged fork and a pot. When he jabbed the tines into the black arm more white bone eased out. On the side of the pot, he wiped the piece of arm off the fork.

"What's happening? I want to know what's happening," the Kid said.

"You saw it; you tell us."

"I saw light, heard noise; I didn't see this," the Kid said, pointing to the pot.

"What do I do with it?" Peewee asked.

"Don't let that Steward see it," the Fat Fireman said.

"Shut up," the Satchel Man said.

"Take it to the messroom, cover it, and put it in the refrigerator for now," the Bosun said.

"Hey, not in our refrigerator."

"No more cold cuts for me."

"Do it," Gus ordered. "Hell, we ate the tongue of a cow last night."

All hands on deck there. The fallout's stopped. The fallout's stopped. All hands on deck back there.

The Chief Mate was coming down the deck, robe streaming. "Fall out, goddamn you."

"Come on," the Bosun said.

"What's all this general quarters crap," the Fat Fireman said. "We ain't had any GQ drill."

They were following the Bosun through the hatchway when the Chief Mate came with clenched fists and outraged voice. "Move, damn your eyes. This is an emergency."

"Look at him," Red said in a low voice. Red was in his skivvies and barefooted. He had been asleep dreaming his mother was coming to wake him when the cloud exploded. "Hee-hee, ain't he something."

"He's aching to hit," Slim the Oiler said, stepping through the hatch and sliding toward the railing away from the outraged Mate.

"A real bucko," Gus whispered.

"Yeah."

"Hits the first man out for not being faster, kicks the last," the Satchel Man said.

"He ain't called Stormy because of those legs," Red said.

"*Stormy Hatton.*" The loudly whispered words floated above their heads as they straggled raggedly up the deck, some wearing clogs, most still in skivvies.

"I heard that," the Chief Mate said in his outraged voice.

"Keep coming," the Bosun said in a low voice.

"Who said that!"

"Keep coming," Gus said.

"Shit, I can take him," Blackie said, finger-combing his silky chest hair.

"It is an emergency," the Bosun said.

"I can still take him," Blackie said.

"Rule book's closed now," Red said.

"Keep coming," Gus said, bumping Blackie, whose eyes flared.

"Keep coming," the Bosun said. "It is our emergency. Look at the ships. It is a big one."

"We'll make port one day," Blackie muttered. "I can wait. Onced I studied waiting at a place for two years two months and twenty-two days. I can do waiting."

They bunched at the bottom of the ladder waiting for the Bosun's one-up and both-on steps to reach the top. The Chief Mate circled their flanks with the robe flapping the snakes and girls and butterflies. "Who called me that?"

Reaching the top of the ladder Blackie turned, silhouetted against the splotched housing. "Mate. You Mate! You going ashore in Joetown?"

The robe swirled, settled around the snakes coiling the Mate's ankles. "Yes, Sailor. I'll be in Joetown. Your name is Blackie? Blackie . . . ?" Holding out the edges of the robe he bowed and smiled. "Blackie. Now move out."

The Bosun looked down into the robe of the Mate. He could see it, but he was too far away to see what was tattooed on it. "Did you see it?" he asked the Kid. "Your eyes are younger."

The Kid covered his head with his arms.

"See what? Where?"

"Come on," the Bosun said.

The ships were in close precise rows, and one of the small gray ships moved from merchantman to merchantman speaking indistinctly over a bullhorn. On a near ship the crew bunched beneath the Captain on their bridge. Their own Captain held the railing of the bridge with both hands. Glinting dully beside his hands a long torn sheet of metal draped the railing like cloth. A last curl of smoke rose from the glinting metal. The gold on the Captain's cap glistened, and it glowed from the golden head on the near ship.

"All right, men. Most of you have been here before. From now until we leave the war zone we stand four on, four off. Twenty-four-hour a day watches for and aft, port and starboard."

The Third Mate appeared on the wing of the bridge. He too had a cap reeven with gold. The two golden heads came secretly together. The Captain's head bobbed as the Third Mate talked. The Third Mate's head bobbed as the Captain talked. Then the two golden heads snapped apart with a thunderous clap. The Third Mate's head disappeared into his shoulders and the Captain's chin popped out rigid. Peewee, followed by his clogs, dove for a hatch with tucking shoulders, and the dartlike plane broke through the gray bottom of the stratus cloud behind the clap of thunder that shook the ship and sent spasms of fear down their bones. The jet screamed over the *Ekonk*, below mast height, made a long slow looping screaming turn, and came slowly back, dipping its dark topped wings first one way and then the other as the tiny pilot searched about, hunting the end of whatever had happened beyond the cloud.

The Third Mate's head eased out of his shoulders. He shook his fist at the plane. "Damn speed demon. Making a lot of damn noise."

"Men," the Captain said over his jutting rigid chin. "Men, a message says two of our planes collided in the cloud. I want these decks cleared. Let's get this junk overboard." The Captain pushed the draped metal from the railing. It clanged on deck at their feet and unfroze them.

"Jesus," Blackie said and someone whistled. Peewee got to his feet and stood with one clog in his hand.

"Come on," the Bosun said. Gus lifted the metal from the deck and, holding it overhead with both hands, braced his feet and tossed it lightly into the sea.

You there, Sailor, knock that off. The small gray ship rushed head-on at them with the numbers 121 black on her bow. A slim khaki shirt rose above the railing of her tiny bridge. Above the shirt the bullhorn was a round red mouth on the top of which sat a golden cap.

Their Captain rushed to the wing end of their bridge, his bullhorn in profile a baby blue growth from his face. *To the captain of the One Two One if you have anything to say to the Ekonk say it to me.*

Your man was throwing wreckage parts overboard.

He was following my orders. We are clearing our decks.

"Quick!" Gus said whirling. "Throw me a piece of anything."

Someone tossed him Peewee's other clog, which he quickly held high out over the side.

You there, Sailor, I said knock that off, squawked the red mouth.

"Hey," Peewee said, "not my clog."

Captain of the One Two One I repeat, if you have any requests to make of the Ekonk you direct them to me and not to my men.

Stop throwing wreckage overboard.

Are you directing that request to me or to my men?

"Goddamnit, Gus," Peewee said.

That is an ORDER. I repeat stop throwing wreckage over the side. We are under orders to gather it for information.

Gus leaned farther out, holding the clog between thumb and forefinger.

To whom was the order directed.

"Gus, goddamnit."

Sailor, don't you drop that.

Sir, I protest your addressing my men directly. I have re-

peatedly asked you to stop and will be compelled to submit a written report of your actions.

"Gus, goddamnit."

Sailor . . . !

The clog turned slowly down from Gus's hand.

"Aw shit," Peewee said.

. . . report this to the convoy commander, squawked the red mouth.

One Two One Captain, are you speaking to me or my men who are under orders to clear my decks? I must repeat that I have requested you again and again to direct your orders to the Captain of this ship. A written report of this will be filed with convoy commander.

Another incident like this and I'll recommend you be removed from the convoy for failure to obey orders, the red mouth yelled.

One Two One Captain, to whom are you addressing your threats?

I am addressing the SS Ekonk, and if you are speaking for the Ekonk, I am addressing you.

I speak for the Ekonk, One Two One, what is your request?

Ekonk, you are ORDERED by the convoy commander to collect all parts of the recent air accident for delivery to the convoy commander.

Thank you One Two One. Your request will be expedited.

Blackie flapped his elbows and ran the deck in circles. "Squawk, squawk, squawk," he said. "Squawk, squawk, squawk."

From the railing Red, skivvies sagging around sinewy legs, said to the Kid, "Hee-hee, gold braid do come out to see itself."

Peewee looked over the rail into the water. "Goddamnit, Gus."

"Shit, Peewee," Gus said turning away. "Wasn't it worth it?"

Red hitched his skivvies. "Way I see it, Kid, we ought to put all the braid everywhere on women with tits aching of milk and hungry kids."

"What?" the Kid said.

Blackie flapped up onto the hatch, and flapped back down again. "Squawksquawksquawk . . ."

"*You there, Sailor.* Stop that." The Captain's two dark eyes peered down over the rim of the baby blue horn.

"Squawk, squawk, squawaa . . ." Blackie circled to a stop and flapped his arms a couple of more times.

The Captain said, "That's it, men. You heard the navy's request. Carry on, Bosun. And get every last scrap. We'll show them how efficient we are." The Captain ducked his golden head at them and disappeared into the wheel house with the Third Mate.

"Bosun!" The Chief Mate stood two decks below the Captain, robe open and legs aspraddle.

"Yessir." The Bosun went to the foot of the ladder and looked up. Then the Bosun mounted the ladder, one foot up both feet on. At the top he leaned back against the railing. "Yessir?"

The Mate didn't look at him. "You heard the Captain, Bosun?"

"Yessir."

"You heard the One Two One request?"

"Yessir."

"Then what are you waiting for?"

"*Your* orders."

The Mate repeated the orders already given the Bosun by

the Captain. ". . . and afterward I want the topside hosed down. I don't want one speck of blood left on this ship."

"Yessir. And what about their breakfast?"

"You didn't let me finish, Bosun. I want you and two others to begin the search now. I want everyone else breakfasted first."

"Yessir."

The Bosun climbed back down the ladders, crooked his finger at the Kid, and said to the Satchel Man, "James, you come with us. Everybody else back to the messroom."

"Hey, godamighty," Peewee said. He was holding out the bottom of his bare foot. The ball and heel were covered with red blood, vermilion. They all looked at their feet. Some clogs were solid with blood, some spotted. Red's feet were only dirty.

"Hell," the Fat Fireman said. "Red's so light he floats. No sea burial for him."

"The flying fish might could eat him," Peewee suggested.

"Hee-hee," Red said leading them back to the messroom. "No blood on my feet."

The Bosun led the Kid and the Satchel Man onto the focslehead. They began gathering, looking everywhere, inside the hawsepipes, behind cleats, inside the anchor winch. They poked into every nook and cranny, and as they found the dark pieces, some no more than jagged slivers, they piled them on deck. The Satchel Man tossed a three-foot-length of copper wiring onto the small pile. "Bosun," he said.

Motioning the Kid back, the Bosun rounded the anchor winch and looked over the Satchel Man's shoulder. "Throw it over the side," the Bosun said.

"Won't they say something?"

"We decide this."

They were looking at a piece of arm almost identical to the one Gus found, except this piece was deeply suntanned.

Bosun, the baby blue mouth called. The Kid and the Satchel Man waited at the railing as the Bosun slowly crossed the deck and disappeared into the housing. He reappeared on the bridge beside the Captain. The *Ekonk* briskly rose and fell and whitecaps broke the gray-blue water. Aloft the breeze whirred inch-and-a-half cables into musical strings, and the ship sang along the wind. When the Bosun came back onto the focslehead, one foot up both feet on, he looked at neither of them. The wind pushed into the back of his gray hair, raising it wild and waving and covering his ears. He had a woven bushel basket in his hand. Like a magician he took from the basket another basket, and then another. "They are for the flesh," he said looking at them. "The navy wants it. They divide what they have into the proper number of coffins. The coffins are sealed and sent to the next of kin."

The Satchel Man's eyes peered from the caves in his hollow face. He tongued his loose front teeth. "They'd get home faster if we fed them to the fish."

The gray hair blew down the Bosun's forehead as he looked toward the cloud. "It was a big one full of soldiers and a little one," he said.

Bosun.

The Bosun climbed back down the ladder and crossed the deck to stand beneath the bridge. The Captain spoke down through cupped hands. The Bosun came back across the deck and climbed the focslehead. He turned his basket upside-down. "The big one full of soldiers," he said and stopped. "The soldiers were black men and white men. We are to put the white meat in one basket, and the black meat in the other. You are the black, Kid. You're the white, James."

"What?" the Kid said.

"You are the black."

"Fish would be faster."

"That reminds me," the Bosun said. "Steward gave me the baskets only if I bring him any flying fish we find." The Bosun turned his basket back over. "I am the fish."

"What?" the Kid said again.

"I am the fish, you are the black, James is the white."

"What are you talking about?" the Kid asked.

"About the next of kin. They are trying to get a part of the body back to the next of kin."

"They're crazy," the Kid said. "You're crazy."

"No," the Satchel Man said. "It makes sense. It'll improve the odds."

"Forget sense, we have got to get these people gathered up," the Bosun said.

"Yes," the Satchel Man said.

"It's our job," the Bosun said.

"What's our job? Putting these things in baskets?" asked the Kid.

"Ship needs clear decks," the Bosun said. "We can't leave these people lying around here."

"I'm talking about putting them in baskets," the Kid said. "I don't know anything about clear decks. Why? Why do you need clear decks? Tell me."

"To walk on," the Bosun said.

"Hah," the Kid said triumphantly. "I ain't going anywhere."

"James, would you step over to the rail and check the water."

Coming back from the railing the Satchel Man said, "We're still forming convoy. I make us about three knots."

"See," the Bosun said to the Kid. "Everything is going somewhere. Without moving a muscle you are three knots for the horizon. And do you know the ocean is moving too? It isn't ever flat. It has holes in its surface, sometimes huge valleys. Sometimes we are all day sailing up the side of a hole. Now let's clear our decks so we can chip and paint and keep this thing moving against the ocean."

They cleaned the focslehead of flesh and metal, and they were on the foredeck when the rest of the crew joined them in a ragged thwartwise line. The Kid and the Satchel Man were no longer searchers but carriers, hauling their baskets back and forth.

"Hey, Kid. You the white?"

"Black."

"I got white."

"Black. Kid! Gimme the black."

"Hurry the black."

"I got a white one."

"Hey, Boats. What about this?"

Gene stood between the hatch and the winch dangling a limp blue-gray length of intestine from the point of his knife.

"Humph!" the Bosun said.

Gene caressed his stomach with his left hand. His translucent skin glowed and the blue-green veins pumped his arms. "Are you going to ask about this one?"

"Humph!" the Bosun said again. "I am afraid to hear what I will be told. I will get another basket. I would rather we do it ourselves than hear it said aloud. Humph!"

Gene dropped the intestine to the deck and sat down on the hatch. "I will be back," the Bosun said, going off with his sliding steps. He came back with another basket. "You are the insides," he said to Gene. "Now hear it, everyone. Gene is the insides, the Kid is the black, James is the white, and I am the flying fish."

"And I am a whale," Red said.

"I need a fucking drink," Gus said.

"A fucking anything," Blackie said, throwing something over the side.

"You are all crazy," the Kid said.

"We are not to throw it over the side," the Bosun said. "It is our job. We do it." He said "Humph!" again and Red came holding by the knee a part of a leg. The flesh was neither black nor white but some indeterminate in-between.

"Which one?" Red asked.

Bosun.

The kneecap before Red's gloved hand whitened. The torn calf gave toward the deck.

Again the Bosun stood beneath the Captain talking down through cupped hands. They all gathered round when the Bosun came back. The Kid had his basket half filled, and he eased it heavily down, looking as startled as a deer at the blood on his thighs. The Satchel Man too had blood on his thighs, and Gene set his basket down and looked inside it shaking his head.

"You will not believe this," the Bosun said.

"Try me," Gene said. "If I can carry around a basket of intestines, livers, and such, it might surprise you what I can believe."

"I don't believe it myself," the Bosun said. "It was three planes. One was theirs. Those we are not sure of," the Bosun said, pointing to the piece of leg Red held outstretched. As the ship moved, the torn calf sought the perpendicular. "Those, they are yellow ones. Some are theirs, some are ours. They have decided upstairs that we are to put half the yellow ones in a basket and throw the other half over the side."

"The fast way," the Satchel Man said.

The Bosun handed yet another basket to Red. "The Kid is the black, James is the white, Gene is the insides, Red is the yellow, and he will tell you when to throw every other one over the side. I am the flying fish."

The Kid kicked over his basket. "I fucking quit," he said.

"You, Kid, you stop using that language," the Satchel Man said.

On the lookout that night, with the ship all hosed down and sparkling clean, the Kid paced the focslehead. He listened to the waves slapping the bow and the wind singing the rigging. He still could hardly believe his ears, *I fucking quit*. He had walked away holding his smarting big toe in the air. Within the close walls of the shower stall, where he stood fully clothed, he had said again through the thickly spraying water, *I quit*. And he was amazed at the ease with which the blood washed down his clothes, down his flesh, his legs, his ankles, between the toes, and down the drain into the sea.

He had stripped off his wet clothes, dropped them in a bucket, and set them bubbling with steam. He paused naked in the dim companionway. The thwartwise line swarmed the midships section, climbed the lifeboats, the splotched wheel house, the housing.

Black here
Over the side or in the basket? Hey Red
Coming white

Gene-boy
Goddamn you, Gus, you call me boy again I'll put YOUR heart in here

With his hair combed wet and tight on his head and with his khakis, cut off at the knees, soft and clean on his hips and thighs, he came back into the companionway to shut off the steam in the bucket. One thin hand rubbed his stomach the way Gene rubbed his, and out in the light Gene was standing on the canvas-topped hold. Against the backdrop of the housing Gene bent to the basket at his feet and dipped his red hands. He flipped out of the basket into the air a snake-long length of entrails. The entrails dropped onto Blackie's back and one end looped his neck. Whirling in a startled crouch, Blackie clawed the flesh from his body and still whirling grabbed the white-flesh basket from the passing Satchel Man and tried to throw the whole bloody mess at Gene. But the basket was too heavy to leave his hands. And still whirling he tried again. With Gene laughing and retreating, Blackie threw the whole basket rolling and spilling flesh across the canvas-topped hold. And all in a motion Blackie came behind it kicking flesh at Gene, who laughed out of reach. In his outrage Blackie began kicking flesh at anyone. The other baskets were dropped, thrown, grabbed, kicked, somehow spilled, and the air was filled with yells, curses, bloody flesh, and three flying fish.

The Kid's fingers dipped over the forming ridges of his stomach. He tightened the ridges. Not bad, he thought, not bad at all.

You men back there, have you gone crazy. Bosun, BOSUN!

He turned off the steam and went back to his bunk.

Later the Satchel Man came into the focsle. He stood silently in the center of the gloomy focsle, head down, eyes staring vacantly from their hollows. Then he shook himself, went to his bunk, and reached for his towel, but his hand fell back empty. He turned and went silently back out on deck.

In his bunk the Kid peeled a loose chip of white paint from the ship's side and laid the tip of his forefinger to the metal. Outside was the water. He was inside. He was supposed to tell the Bosun about the places where the paint was peeling, where the rust was growing beneath the paint. They chipped it away and painted the weakened metal with red lead. *Red.* He began to shake. His arms and shoulders chilled, and he hugged himself into a tight ball and pressed his cheek to the metal plate separating him from the sea. He could feel the water moving against the ship's side, feel the propeller pound the water, hear the thrusting engine, the hundred gurgling pipes, the stretch and give of metal plates, even hear the wind and the sound of voices and hammering and footsteps.

And he slept. He willed it.

He rocked in a dream of riding a bed of hay in his grandfather's slow creaking wagon. And in his dream his grandfather was, as always, a huge piece of striped peppermint candy. At the age of four he looked up at his grandfather, past the silver belt graven with the head of a bull, way up there where his grandfather lived, and he hollered, "Grandpa, when you gonna die?"

The silver bull shook with laughter, and his grandfather said in his roaring voice, "I'm going to live to be a hunnert, Boy, then turn into something good to eat." Right then, standing before his very eyes, his grandfather had turned into striped peppermint candy, silver buckle, bull horns,

and all. And all that next year before his grandfather was
kicked to death by a mule, they rode in the wagon together,
fished together, walked together, and he walked and rode
and fished with a peppermint man. He looked into the peppermint eyes and laughed, because nobody in the world had
a better grandpa than he had. He could hardly wait. And
his grandfather told his father, "You know, sometimes the
way that boy looks at me makes my hair stand."

And he awoke. He didn't will it.

He awoke with his cheek pressed in an ache to the metal
side, to the sea rocking the ship, and to the shouts of the
crew coming into the focsle. They were all drenched to the
skin, some naked, all shouting and happily slapping each
other with wet shirts or dungarees. They snapped salty
sprays into his bunk, and the droplets fell cool on his face.

"Get him. He fucking quits."

"And got away with it," Gene said.

"Because he's a stupid kid."

"No," Gene said. "No, he told them to shove it. The
Mate himself couldn't have got him back out there. The
Kid's O.K."

"Can you imagine the old man thought *we* were crazy."

"Drunken slob."

"Takes the shore to get him on deck."

He climbed from his bunk and without a word walked
through them. The decks were still wet. They had hosed
down the whole ship. The only traces of blood were on the
ship's sides beneath the scuppers. It clung dark and red,
and the first weather would wash it to the ocean.

Near the housing the Bosun, the Chief Mate, the Satchel
Man, and the baskets squatted in a circle around the flesh
heaped on the deck. The Satchel Man was putting it back
in the baskets. The Bosun and the Mate watched. The

Satchel Man was on his knees, his face a painted mask. With bloody hands he picked the pieces from the pile, inspected them, and laid them in the appropriate baskets.

He passed the trio without a word. He went to the bow to get as far away from them as he could. Then he went to the foremast and climbed to the crosstree. He sat in the sky. One time the Bosun came and stood at the railing looking up. He knew it was the first part of his watch and time for him and the Bosun to paint, splice line, or do whatever the ship needed the two of them to do. But he sat leaning against the mast until the sun went down, then he climbed down and paced the focslehead on lookout, knowing for the first time in his life he had limits that had nothing to do with the strength and the skill of his forming muscles

2

CAPTAIN'S LOG

July 17: Made this day 182 miles. Joined convoy at 04:48 hours. Captain of the Escort Vessel 121 persisted in bypassing me and ordering my men directly in spite of my repeatedly calling his attention to his error. I have written a protest to be delivered to the convoy commander. Picked up from the decks following an explosion at 05:20 hours as follows:

1 basket caucasian flesh 12 lbs.
1 basket negroid flesh 27 lbs.
1 basket mongoloid flesh 22 lbs.
1 basket unidentified flesh 12 lbs.
metal 116 lbs.

The flesh has been stored in the fish box at 2°.

3

Four days and four nights they rode their convoy station.
The Captains blinked at each other in the night and flagged
each other in the day. Maritime law was strictly observed.
The Kid stood his watches and wondered what he was
watching for. They told him to watch for torpedo wakes.

Torpedo *wakes*. First things first, he said, teach me submarines.

He never did learn submarines, but he learned torpedo
wakes. He sat on a hatch on lookout early one morning.
Red prowled up out of the darkness to sit beside him. They
stared silently into the night sea elbows on knees, and he
was thinking about blood when Red stiffened beside him.
Red's stiff palms pushed air, and his mouth opened in a
voiceless scream.

"What?" the Kid said.

Air hiccupped Red's open throat. He looked down Red's
outstretched arms, sighted, and there it was. In the water.
A path streaked out of the night sea and disappeared beneath the railing at their feet. The torpedo was even now
nosing into the ship.

"God shit," Red said.

"What?" the Kid said.

"I thought . . ."

They lifted each other to their feet.

From where they sat the horizontal boom in its collar
had blotted out the horizon and the edge of moon rising
above it. They had been looking underneath the boom at
the moon's path.

"Thought they had me," Red said.

So he learned torpedo wakes looked like moon streaks.

But by the time they reached port he still didn't know submarines. The land mass formed out of the dark water, and the convoy slowed. One by one the ships pushed up a river that opened into an elongated bay of dark water and anchored ships. The bay was surrounded by low green land. In the distance a brown mountain hung behind the mile-long row of continuous docks, ships, and warehouses. High above the warehouses banks of lights hung on poles. The block-long warehouses glistened navy gray and clean. From the navy gray front of the center warehouse huge black letters proclaimed:

WAR IS OUR BUSINESS
BUSINESS IS GOOD

They were still tightening the lines to the dock when word was passed from the Bosun that, as usual here, there would be no shore leave.

Gene wrapped a hawser over itself on the winch drum and pulled the ship into the dock with only the muscle it took to lift the loop of line. "It'll be a long three days," he said to the Kid flaking the line beside him.

"I didn't come all this way not to see," the Kid said.

"You'll have a grandstand seat. Required attendance. HiYUH hiYUH, step right up, ladies and gentlemen! See the frogmen in action. Watch the rockets come off the mountain. Hear the ship go BOOM! HiYUH hiYUH, ladies and gentlemen, the Kid says he came to see the greatest fireworks show the world has ever seen! Free, absolutely free, ladies and gentlemen, not one tenth of a dollar. But FREE with the compliments of the taxpayers!"

"Really?" the Kid said.

"You know why you can't go ashore?" Gene said. "It's because of them."

The Kid's eyes swept the dock crowded with longshoremen pouring in and out of the warehouses. "Them?"

"So what do they look like?" Gene asked.

The Kid flaked line and studied the dock. The longshoremen wore everything from full military uniforms to loincloths. American uniforms walked the dock among them, a full head taller. The smaller men had browned bodies and moon-round faces. The Kid turned back to Gene.

"So?"

"So can you tell them apart?"

"I can tell the American soldiers."

"Not enough. Those others, some are on our side, some the other. That's why you can't go ashore. You can't tell the friendlies from the enemies."

The coil of hawser slipped on the drum. Gene flipped on another loop and leaned against the new loop talking. "Hasn't anybody told you why you have to know who's who?"

"No."

"Some people don't know anything. When our first heaving line hit the dock it rang a price on your head."

Gene leaned back holding the hawser and looked past the Kid to the dock. "See that one. The skinny little bastard in the torn skivvies on the bollard. See him? He's got maybe to his name those dirty skivvies and a muzzle-loading piece of pipe he calls a rifle hid in the bush. Know what fifty dollars would mean to him? That heaving line put a fifty-dollar price on the heads of every sailor aboard. Officers run a little higher, though. Look up there."

The Captain leaned on the bridge railing with the Chief Mate.

"Those two run fifteen hundred apiece. Thirty times your flesh."

"I'll take mine," the Kid said.

"Step right up, ladies and gentlemen, and take it! Flesh for sale. Sale or rent. What's your pleasure? By the hour, night, month, or year. On the slab or in the crib. Listen, Kid, flesh is always on the cheap, even at fifteen hundred a head, step right up, ladies and gentlemen, you think you got problems? You wanta get away from it all? Step right up and watch the Johns get into the meat to get outta the flesh. Listen, Kid, one thing I'll tell you, the next time I sign on for a little trip to get out of the house, I'm not by God going through a war zone."

"What are you talking about?"

"I'm talking about selling your life for fifty dollars when I know a girl likes to smell Aqua Velva, just about your age, in Galveston turns twice that a night."

"You mean a whore."

The Kid stopped the hawser with a double and two single half hitches. Gene nodded approval and let the hawser's tension tighten the Kid's knots, then he looped the hawser around the bollards.

"Watch the way you say whore, Kid. They're the only ones don't deal in the flesh. They deal in the spirit only. You know anybody else can sell an empty hole and have a satisfied customer?"

Walking aft after finishing tying up, Gene called the Kid to the railing. "Hey, you said you came to see. Look at that sight."

Triangles of brightly colored sails blew from a partly hidden cove. The lead boat, under a striped red-and-white sail, rounded the hulk of a partly sunken ship and headed smartly up the bay. Inside the cove a stretch of white sand separated the jungle green from the dark water. Red and green and orange and yellow parasols stuck like lollipops from the sand and brown oily bodies sprawled beneath the parasols. A red-bikinied girl popped from beneath an orange parasol and fled for the water chased by two slim brown men.

Behind the crescent beach stood a row of four large square buildings. "It's an R and R area," Gene said. "That beach is strictly from Florida. Six shiploads of Florida sand. Make you feel at home?"

"Never been to Florida," the Kid said.

"But you've dreamed it and there it is, every American's dream, Miami Beach on Long Song Bay. And with showgirls! What would Miami Beach be without girls. I myself last year put together a 'dance' group from Galveston. Like Miami Beach this place gets its girls from all over. Hometown stuff for the boys. I booked the best fifteen girls from Galveston, six weeks into Long Song Bay. Aqua Velva said it was the best fucking time she ever had. The hotels are the Northeast, Southeast, Midwest, and West. The rooms are named for cities in those places. Every soldier stays in the city nearest his hometown in good ole U.S.A. And mixed in with the six shiploads of Florida sand is a bucketful from every famous beach in the world. How about them fish?"

"How's the swimming?"

"Stupid Kid," Gene said laughing. "Look at 'em go."

The sailboats rounded the bow of a black tanker leaning back on its anchor chain. They watched the bright sails tilt briskly among the anchored ships.

"Hey Kid, you say you wanta know how the swimming is? Let's hit the other side."

Dockside the Bosun directed the placing of the gangway. At the foot of the gangway a hundred tiny longshoremen waited for the Bosun's *all clear*.

"There they are," Gene said.

Where, the Kid was about to say when the air shook with a continuous roll of thunder. On the distant mountain bright flowers of earth splashed upward. They bloomed on one end of the mountain, grew smoothly atop the mountain's brown length, and stopped blooming at the other end. For a moment the blooms held, then the earth sank back. The mountain became a halo around itself, then the wind smeared the halo into a haze. Tiny flashes of sunlight spurted back toward the sea.

"How can they see?" Gene asked in wonder.

"It's done by numbers," the Kid said. "I read it. They never look down. They look at dials, and when those dials all get just right the doors pop open and down it comes."

"They've been killing that mountain since my first trip here," Gene said. "They'd just made this place into a war zone. You could walk around out there then. We even went hunting. Too many things to step on now, and the mountain was green then. They browned her with spray a year ago. There," Gene said pointing. "That answer your question about swimming?"

Out of the center warehouse marched three uneven lines of men with black masks pushed back on their heads and silver tanks strapped to their backs. They kneed the air with black-flippered feet. Each had a knife and a light belted to his waist and each carried a black spear gun. American flags shone from the black rubber suits. Their leader lined them in three orderly rows along the warehouse as the Bosun signaled an all clear to the longshoremen. The gangway filled with the tiny longshoremen who spread all over the ship. Hatches popped open, steam hit the winches, and the three orderly rows of spearmen, on signal, shook the air with their spears. They masked their faces, pushed in their mouthpieces, and all crooked watch-strapped left arms in front of their masks.

Again they shook their spears and split into two-man teams. Two by two they kneed to the edge of the dock and two by two leaped to the water. A short way down the dock two black-masked men, each carrying a black spear and a light and knife and wearing black flippers and a black rubber suit with an American flag, climbed from the water onto the dock. As they kneed dripping across the dock, two more climbed out. And as two more climbed out and entered the warehouse, two more leaped to the water.

"They take their swimming seriously here," Gene said.

"I don't see how that's so serious. They're hardly staying in long enough to get wet," the Kid said.

"What . . ." Gene said.

"If I went to all that trouble getting dressed, I'd like to stay in a little longer," the Kid said.

"Holy mother! You mean you . . . Hell, Kid, those getting out aren't the ones getting in."

"No?"

"They're changing our guard."

"Oh."

"They've been in for hours."

"Oh."

"I start thinking you're O.K., and you pull something worse than any dumb-assed Kid I ever shipped with."

"It's what I saw," the Kid said. "Two jumped in, two exact same ones climbed out. Why shouldn't I believe what I see? I don't know how else to do it."

"They're frogmen, Kid. They swim day and night under all these ships to keep the other side from pinning mines to us and kapowing half the harbor. They're frogmen."

"They look it," the Kid said.

"Come on, Kid. Let's get some more time and a half, and you wait till dark to see what the frogmen do. There goes the first slingful."

They stopped to watch the load of bombs arc from the hold and over the side.

"I've never been too thrilled carrying bombs," Gene said. "I've wanted those babies off ever since they came aboard."

"Ha!" the Kid said. "Well, hello, stupid."

"What's the matter with you?"

"You mean you think those bombs you see coming out are the ones you saw going in? It seems to me if we got one stupid around here we got to learn to count to two."

"Stupid Kid," Gene said laughing. "You'll get your brains kicked in some day. Come on, Red's on the bow with binoculars. After we help the Bosun tie those lighters and barges alongside we'll go look through Red's glasses and see something else not to believe in."

Crossing back to the other side they went behind a tiny winchman sitting behind his winch on his private box. The box had a thin cushion nailed on top and AMPONIC INTERNATIONAL stamped on the side.

Gus was still tightening a line from the barge when a sling of bombs lowered into the half-naked men on the barge's deck. The Bosun looking down over the railing hand-signaled through the clatter of winches, and Gus lashed the line to a cleat.

"What do you think of the barges, Boats?" Gene asked.

"I think it is a good idea. The sooner and farther we are from the bombs the better."

"Course it's good," Gus said. "All they've got to do up there is plan and stuff. I wonder why they didn't think of it sooner. Why unload them on the dock and have us sit beside them for three days. Barge them the hell away soon as they're off. Great idea. At last we know somebody up there's doing what he's paid to do — think."

4

The golden caps of the Port Captain and the *Ekonk* Captain glinted sunlight from the bridge of the *Ekonk*.

They left the bridge and entered the Captain's cabin.

"Jim," the Port Captain said, waving his arms around the cabin. "Here you have to think BIG."

The Port Captain swiveled at the *Ekonk*'s Captain's desk while the *Ekonk* Captain mixed drinks in the bathroom. The Port Captain was all hairy. Hair tufted from his ears and nose and grew over his open shirt collar. He slid the golden cap off his bald brown head. "Everything out here is big, Jim. We're only reaching our growth potential. Soon we'll be supporting a million men. And this one will last for years."

The *Ekonk* Captain's golden head rounded the door. "We need to lay plans then. Did you do the thing I wrote about?"

The Port Captain tugged the hair in his ear. "Best ones I've ever seen. And only the beginning."

The *Ekonk* Captain brought out two tall brown glasses.

"What'll it be this time?" the Port Captain asked.

"Health," the *Ekonk* Captain said. "Let's drink to health."

They clicked glasses.

The continuous roll of thunder filled the cabin.

"We're making one last try on the mountain," the Port Captain said. "Damned nuisance. They got one last month, you know. Pure luck. In spite of all precautions they rocket a garbage can of explosives at us every three or four days. And last month they hit one — ammo ship. I thought the whole port had blown. Tomorrow we're hitting the mountain one last time, comb it good, and if it fails, what we're going to do is beautiful."

"Big?"

"It has to be finalized in Washington. If tomorrow doesn't stop these people from lobbing rockets, they are *finished*."

The Port Captain laid a brown leather pouch on the desk and squeezed from it two midnight-blue eggs. "There you are. How about that for star sapphires?"

The *Ekonk* Captain turned them in his hand. "Perfect. Absolutely perfect."

"You say perfect. Here's the perfection." The Port Captain placed a brown paper bag on the desk and peeled the paper from a stone man, sitting fat and contented, with vacant holes for eyes. The Port Captain fitted the huge sapphires into the eye sockets. "He's said to see through heaven."

"And as a work of art he can go through customs."

"And no gimmick. He's a real idol and those are his real eyes. Idols like that are all over this country. Authentic works of primitive art."

"All waiting for gem eyeballs," the *Ekonk* Captain said, taking the empty glasses into the bathroom. "Superb."

Again the thunder rolled through the cabin.

"If tomorrow isn't successful, the plan is this. You know

the old dream in this country of damming the river to this bay. Well that's it. If tomorrow fails, we're pushing the damned mountain into the river. We'll stop the rockets, and we'll stop their frogmen from floating mines down on us. Here's how we're selling it. The Pentagon is buying because we lost another ship. And the Pentagon can sell it to the hill because the hill can sell it to the voters as a do-gooder reclamation project. It will help ease our image of ourselves and make it easier to sell the war."

"And the bay?"

"Without the river we'll have to abandon the bay, and that's another beautiful part. *Look what we're sacrificing to build you this dam.* It proves we view our bases here as temporary. But down the coast is another mountain we're having trouble with. We're going to move that mountain into the ocean and make exactly the kind of bay we need. Maybe we could buy the dirt by the cubic yard and build it outside the three-mile limit, make it really ours. Or does dirt always remain a part of the nation it comes from? We're looking into that."

"Is all this your planning?"

"A modest part. I'm still only learning to have the big ideas. It's hard to get accustomed to. But it can be learned, Jim, and you should learn it. Everybody's in competition on the little ideas, but only a handful are in there fighting on the big ones. And when we leave this country we can be proud. We'll change it forever. A new bay built to perfection. More power than will be needed in the foreseeable future. Farm water by tap. What do you think?"

"I'm not sure I can learn it," the *Ekonk* Captain said.

"Abandoning the bay means building a new R and R area. Now think about *that*."

"And money's no object. Think of it this way: what makes an R and R area in civilian life?"

The *Ekonk* Captain pushed the golden cap to the back of his head and realized he hadn't realized civilian life had R and R areas.

"Keep thinking about it. I myself got the idea last time I was back home driving through Nashville, Tennessee. At about zero three hundred hours I drove around a corner and there in the dark all shining with light, you know what I saw?"

The *Ekonk* Captain shook his head.

"I saw ahead of me in Nashville, Tennessee" — the Port Captain's voice dropped to a whisper — "the Parthenon."

The Port Captain leaned forward, waiting, with the hair tufting out each ear.

"Do you see it often?" the *Ekonk* Captain asked.

"No, no. I mean really. No, not really. I mean I really saw a replica of it."

"You saw stones and all?"

"It's really there, in Nashville, a replica of the Parthenon."

"Oh."

"*Why* is it there is the question," the Port Captain said.

"I didn't until now know it *was* there."

"Well, why do tourists go to Athens. Same reason."

"Yes . . . ?"

"They go to see the Parthenon. And why do they go to Rome?"

"To see the Coliseum?" asked the *Ekonk* Captain.

"Right. And they go to Pisa . . . ?"

"To see the tower."

"Now you're doing it."

"But what am I doing?"

"Big, Jim. Think BIG. If a one-horse town like Nashville can build the Parthenon, what could the combined armed forces do? We'll duplicate all the great tourist attractions of the world. And we can use the things for practical purposes. Imagine for a moment the Leaning Tower of Pisa, now get this, a hotel! Private rooms below and on the very top, a lookout tower. Or maybe a machine gun emplacement. Confidentially, Jim, it'll go regardless of the mountain. Since we need another hotel, it'll go on the Florida sand."

The Port Captain yanked hair from his ear.

"Imagine. An R and R camp civilians would pay to see. We'd have to put in extra hotels."

The roll of thunder filled the cabin.

"Of course we could never make the thing self-supporting. It cost us between four and five million to put that load of bombs on the mountain. But with slot machines, food and drink, and entrance fees, we could turn a healthy sum for the Rec Department. And when we leave we could turn the whole shebang over to the host country. A ready-made tourist attraction. When this all stops and we start building the country back, it will help our taxpayers put this country back on its feet."

He yanked hair from his right nostril, and the *Ekonk* Captain suddenly said, "My God, what about the pyramids?"

"We've worked on those, Jim. Too Big. We'll do the Sphinx, to scale of course. We could do the pyramids to scale, but the whole thing with pyramids is size. Can you imagine a pyramid only fifty feet high? Nothing. Strictly from nothing."

The *Ekonk* Captain reached for the other's glass, but the Port Captain put his hand over the top. "I have to get back to the office." At the door of the cabin, they shock hands. "And I'm pleased, Jim, to see you can now have a couple of leisurely drinks without . . . I was worried about going partners in this thing."

"I know when to drink now."

At the door of the cabin they shook hands.

"There he sits," the Port Captain said.

They both looked at the idol on the desk.

"Sees through heaven and goes through customs. Either way is a long way in any man's world. I'll get back to you, Jim."

The *Ekonk* Captain closed the door and cleaned the brown glasses in the sink. Leisurely drinks and quit, hell. His had been plain water. He lay back on his bunk and tried to think. On the ceiling he saw the word BIG. Then he found the idol staring at him through starry midnight-blue eyes. That was good about lessening the competition. For every Port Captain there were hundreds of ship captains.

But he had to face it. He would never have envisioned, even remotely, turning an R and R area into a tourist site. The Florida sand had overwhelmed him. He lay on his side looking into the eyes that saw through heaven until he grew drowsy. His eyes closed.

WAR IS OUR BUSINESS
BUSINESS IS GOOD

A tourist site.

His eyes popped wide-open, and he came upright without moving a muscle.

He saw it all. The whole war — a tourist site!

The biggest fireworks show on earth. See the bombs bursting, not on television or in the movies, but in the field.

Politicians and newsmen got to see it. And entertainers. Entertainers went home touting war and bragging and wearing uniforms. One old whatsisname made it a career, wore a uniform with rows and rows of medals and sold war all over television. But they had to make money out of it afterward. He'd make it on the spot. He'd make this Everyman's War. Cut out the middleman, let the tourists see firsthand.

See firsthand your son's war!

The parents alone meant two million tourists. He saw fleets of ships and planes streaming back and forth from the States. Tourists in hats ate and drank, pulled slot machine handles, and snapped pictures of the dead.

Two million?

It could easily pull ten, even twenty million a year.

Business is good, *hell*. He'd be the first man in history to make actual war pay!

5

The Kid waited for dark to see what the frogmen did, but dark didn't come. When the sun went down, the banks of incandescent lights brightened the bay by the thousands.

The barges stayed alongside, loaded now with bombs.

"When are they going to move them?" the Kid asked Gene in the incandescent glare. "And how come we stand lookout in port? Do they think one of these tied-up ships is going to run into one of the anchored ones?"

"It's called gangway watch," Gene said.

"Then why aren't we on the other side watching it?"

"Because we've got more important things to watch. It's

just *called* gangway watch. You keep looking out there."

"But I don't know what I'm looking for."

"I told you — sticks."

"Sticks," the Kid repeated. "We're standing gangway watch on the side of the ship the gangway isn't on looking for sticks sticking out the water. Hell."

"Watch the language or the Satchel Man will get you. And go forward and ease the bow line. I'll get the spring and stern. And ease it well. We don't want the tide to part a line with the damn barges tied to us, and your guess is as good as mine."

"Guess what?"

"Damnit, why do you ask questions anyway. *When* they're moving the barges. Now let's ease 'em, and when we get back, maybe you can see firsthand which sticks."

The Kid went forward and sagged an arc into the line to the dock. When he came back, Gene was at the dockside railing. "Over here, Kid."

On the edge of the dock two teams of black-suited frogmen hauled at a rope like fishermen. But instead of a fish they hauled out a dripping brown body. One of the frogmen one-handed the body onto the dock, where it lay on its side with its knees up.

"What's that on his face?" the Kid asked.

"His breathing reed," Gene said.

One of the frogmen ripped tape from the small face, and the reed came with it.

"He's only a little kid," the Kid said.

"Little or big, he can still blow our asses over the warehouse. Now you know frogmen and sticks."

Peewee came out on deck in his skivvies rubbing his tiny mustache. He waved at them and looked nervously at the barges. "I thought so," he said coming back. "Now we're twice as big a target. It's a good idea, nothing's done. It's something shitty, we got enforcers everywhere."

"Listen to the perfect messboy," Gene said. "Come on, Kid, let's get back on watch now that you know what you're watching for."

"I want to watch here a while," the Kid said looking at the small brown body. And he stood at the railing until it was time to go off watch. Then he and Gene went into the dark focsle. They slept and before dawn took up the watch again. On the dock another brown body lay beside the first.

The roll of thunder shook the air, and in the darkness beyond the lights splintered flowers flamed on the mountain. The planes droned away. A single helicopter whumped through the darkness above the lights. Its sound beelined for the mountain.

"Well," Gene said. "We're going to see us a real sight come sunup. You ever before had a ringside seat to a live bout? You hang on here while I go aft and reliberate those big glasses Red liberated when the Japs were the bad yellows."

Gene was a long time returning, and when he did the crew came with him, coffee cups in hand. The crew crowded the focslehead and the officers crowded the bridge. Red sat in a cushioned rocker with his hands over the big glasses covering his lap.

"Gene," Red said, "you will look last."

"Oh go to hell. If you hadn't caught me lifting them, you wouldn't even know it was happening. And don't threaten me or I'll drop you and the glasses both over the side."

"Here come the helicopters," Blackie said.

The helicopters rose from the green jungle like a school of

fish. They nosed into formation and hung in the morning air above the green growth.

Gus didn't take his eyes from the helicopters grouping now into sections of v's. "Lives in a whorehouse. Fights in rings. Everything safe."

"I've won more than I've lost," Gene said rubbing his ridged stomach. "Fifteen wins, eight losses to be exact."

Gus lifted thick arms and shook dangling limp fingers. "I'm trembly scared." His hands dropped. "Remember when we get at it, there won't be any gloves."

"And we will get at it," Gene said giving a short laugh. "You and me, Gus, we are bound to get at it."

"All right," the Bosun said. "We cannot watch more than one fight at a time."

The helicopters roar filled the bowl of the bay. The lead helicopter broke away, and one by one the others lifted their tails and followed. Overhead they saw the gun muzzles and the doll men behind them.

"Hey, they're gunships."

The air was filled with clattering balloons of drifting steam and swinging loads of bombs and beer and toilet paper. At the mountain the string of gunships made a right-angle turn, and suddenly they all had smoky tails. Chains of bright-red balls floated down to the mountain as a low angry bellow filled the bay. The lead craft swung on its red chain behind the mountain and the others followed.

At regular intervals the helicopters disappeared around one end and appeared at the other end.

On the bridge the officers leaned their elbows on the railing, held their glasses to their eyes, and cheered.

"Yea, team. *Go*, bombers," Slim the Oiler said.

"How do you mean that *go?*"

"Help yourself to any way you want to take it or not take it."

"All right," Red said handing the glasses to the Bosun. "You are first."

"Look," the Kid said. "The red balls are coming the other way."

They curved up from a huge rock below the edge of the rim. A gunship slid to one side, belched black smoke, and skittered sideways into the wall of mountain. It stuck there like a long-legged spider.

"I can't see what is holding it," the Bosun said, "but one of the men is getting out."

A cheer rose from the bridge.

The long-legged helicopter slid downward, then stopped. Then it slid again and dropped slowly down the face of the mountain and disappeared into the green below.

Across the bay suntanned men in bathing suits stuck orange and red and yellow parasols into the white Florida sand. Two couples played at the water's edge with a black-and-white Frisbee. A powerboat towed a wooden tower from the partially hidden cove. The boat tugged the tower into place off the white beach and anchored it.

Around the mountain the circle of helicopters stopped. They gathered like inquisitive fish, and falling chains of red balls entangled the rock.

A red-crossed helicopter rose from the green jungle and raced the bay gaining altitude. As it raced for the mountain, the gunships formed into two circles. The large circle circled the mountain, and the small one circled the man on the mountainside. The small circle fired red balls into the rock. The red-crossed helicopter slid beneath the small circle, and a ladder dropped from its bottom.

"The man's wedged in the rocks," the Bosun said.

Red balls floated up from the big rock, and the red-crossed helicopter slid away. Again the rock was tangled with red chains.

The red-crossed helicopter slid back beneath the small circle. Again the ladder dropped. A single chain of red balls floated up. Sucking up its ladder, the red-crossed helicopter slid out. Each time it eased toward the mountain and lowered the ladder, red balls rose from the rock.

In the cove coconut-oiled bodies came from beneath the bright parasols and swam out to the diving platform. They swanned and jackknifed over the water, then swam back to the tower to dangle their legs in the water or sprawl in the sun.

The short Steward, with his fat hidden muscles, balanced a large tray of cookies and sandwiches onto the bridge. The officers drank coffee, chewed cookies, and watched the mountain through their glasses.

Peewee left the focslehead and came back with a two-gallon bucket of coffee. "Hell, I ought to hawk it," he said filling their cups with a dipper.

From the cove a covey of sailboats tilted triangular sails downwind for the sunken hulk. The blackened lifeguard atop the tower jumped up to wave his red warning flag at a distant swimmer.

On the mountain the rock was slippery with ricocheting red balls.

Unmolested now the red-crossed helicopter leisurely dropped the ladder. As the ladder wound down, red balls rose from a clump of brown trees. The helicopter slid away and continued sliding. Trailing light smoke, it gulped its ladder, slid slowly back to the bay, clattered overhead, and sank into the jungle.

"Their number two boy shoots real good," Red said.

Another red-crossed helicopter rose from the jungle and hurried toward the mountain.

"Here we go again."

The black-suited frogmen marched from the warehouse, kneed across the dock, and leaped off. Other pairs climbed out of the water and kneed into the warehouse. Alongside the *Ekonk* empty barges were towed up and inserted between the *Ekonk* and the filled barges. Cargo platforms of bombs swung seaward to the barges, and cargo nets of beer and toilet paper swung to the dock. The beer was hand-carried into the warehouse. The nets of toilet paper dropped directly into the beds of six-by trucks. The loaded trucks crawled down the dock, rounded the corner, and disappeared into the dust of the previous truck.

Peewee skipped down the focslehead ladder and dodged among the swinging loads. He carried another bucket of coffee and a bucket of sandwiches: liverwurst, boiled tongue, and a sausage made of the cheeks and lips of hogs stuffed inside their own intestines.

"Hey, Peewee, you missed it. They got another helicopter, and we got their number one gunner," Red said rearing back in the rocker.

"Yeah," Gene said. "We get a guy; they get a chopper. Anybody want to bet on Detroit against the Ginks?"

Red said, "Look, it's coming from the big rock again."

"Then we didn't get him after all," Gene said to Gus.

"Did too. And we'll get this new one," Gus said.

Peewee stuck one of his buckets inside the other and from the head of the ladder, he looked at them perched around the focslehead drinking coffee and eating sandwiches. "Well by God if you think I'm serving lunch here you got another one coming."

✿

The Chief Mate pushed off the bridge railing and stuck his elbow in the Third Mate's ribs.

"Sorry."

With his binoculars swinging at his neck and his kimono flowing, he slid on his palms down the bridge ladder If the Third had said one more time *Look at the damn nuts* he wouldn't have been responsible. No man had to listen to that. He swirled the tail of his robe into the shadows of his room and sprawled tattooed legs from the swivel chair.

The worst part of a Chief Mate's job was no action. The best part was in emergency he was free. The bastard on that mountain was no quitter. He had come out that chopper door, grabbed the mountain wall, and pulled himself into it. Now he lay up there alone in a crevice waiting his chance to live.

The Chief's heart hammered, and his whole body trembled. He surged upright in the chair, gripping its arms. In the shadows he felt all the ship in his hands. Christ for somebody to hit, pound with his fists, smash his body into.

The night he broke his legs he was the one they turned to. The loose anchor pounded the *Caleche's* bow, and they'd waited for the hull to cave in. And they waited for him. The gray-faced Captain clung to the chart table in the dark and shadowless wheel house. He stood at the pitching wheel and watched the Captain across the heads of the old mates and bosun staggering in a circle with their arms around each other.

"Well?" the Captain hollered above the roar of the wind and the cannonading of steel on water.

The *Caleche's* bow nosed off-angle into the base of a wave and disappeared. He spun the spokes to catch her lunge beneath the water. The bow nosed out of the wave at a forty-five-degree angle. The loose anchor hung in the air and swung into the *Caleche's* side. The throb of the anchor's weight against the hull touched his feet. Wind and water moaned in around the edges of the door.

"Well?"

The movement of the ship stepped him off the sea grating and walked him past the staggering circle. The Second Mate's face split into curses as he grabbed the wheel and climbed over the spokes onto the grating.

With his hand on the door handle he looked at the Captain.

"Two troughs," he hollered at the Captain. "Try to give me two." The door sucked from his hand. He and some charts blew onto the wing of the bridge.

Immediately he was wet to the skin. Two gray-haired mates fought the door, and he clung to the bridge railing in a roar of wind. Cloud bottom was all around him. Black tendrils blew into the mountainous waves. Salty rain rode the wind. It blew into the sides of the waves and back off the tops. The dark air was thin and hard to get, and he felt he was suffocating. The *Caleche's* bow dropped and, with an explosive crack, disappeared. His knees bent. Dark-green water rolled against the bridge as the decks disappeared. Then the bow rose free. In a stumbling rush he was down the bridge ladder and inside the housing slapping the dogs behind him.

His shoulders bounced from bulkhead to bulkhead through the housing companionways. At times he leaned forward pulling, climbing the deck with bent knees, at times he stiffened his legs to keep from running. He turned corners and stopped before another dogged door. When he loosened all the dogs except one, water poured the door's edges.

He threw his wet clothes to the deck. His scar-new tattoos of yellow and red birds and butterflies and girls and flowers glistened as the *Caleche* rose from the water and he cracked the door. Beside the door an inch-and-a-half manila lifeline quivered and sang the wind. The lifeline ran from a cleat beside the door to the focslehead ladder across the deck. There the lifeline ended. The bow dug into the next wave, and he quickly dogged shut the door. From the bulkhead he took a fire ax, wondering as he did what he would need it for. He stripped the belt from the dungarees and belted the ax to the small of his back. He pulled it free then stuck it back again and waited in the dark for the *Caleche* to rise.

Shoving open the hatch, he stepped out onto the wet deck. A stringy black cloud blew over the coming wave and smashed, turning, into the housing. He grabbed the lifeline and braced his back to the bulkhead as the bow dug at the base of a wave. A wall of green water washed down deck. He took a deep breath and ducked. The water hit him, warm as fresh milk, and pounded him against the bulkhead. He clung to the jerking lifeline wondering if it would hold.

The water stopped beating him against the bulkhead, but he couldn't find his feet. He hung white-knuckled in washing, hip-deep water. The scuppers spouted, and when his left foot caught the deck, he ran hand-over-hand through the wash.

A sheet of spume blew from the crest of the next wave, high as a ten-story building. He had seen a messboy with a bucket of soup in either hand caught once by a wave. The boy hurled soup, bucket, and himself at the wave as though he would destroy it.

Ducking his head he leaped with the lifeline against the falling green water. Flowers and birds and butterflies and girls filled his eyes, and warm salty water poured into his mouth and nose.

When he came out of the wave the ax was gone, and his skivvies hung on one foot. He ran hand-over-hand for the focslehead ladder kicking at the skivvies and spitting saltwater.

He ducked in behind the focslehead ladder and peered out between laddered bars. The anchor throbbed the hull, and the deck jarred his bones. The ship dug in and a wave poured overhead. Beneath the ladder, with his back to the bulkhead, green seawater rushed overhead. He stood in a pocket of air and for the first time could really breathe. The wind no longer roared. Solid water separated him from the wind. He looked up into his green sky and saw the darkness beneath the water the same as the darkness above.

Then the roar of the wind hit his ears as his ocean sky thinned. On the wheel-house glass the watery Captain waved at him in midday darkness. The ship swung her head slowly away from the line of waves. Again the water poured over the focslehead and rolled over him. Again he stood in his pocket of air breathing slowly. He hitched the belt around his naked waist and stuck a tentative finger into the overhead sea. The water knocked it back.

As the water thinned, he climbed the ladder through the drops. The *Caleche* hung halfway down the side of a mountain. The anchor throbbed, and he crawled on hands and knees across the tilted deck, climbed into and out of the anchor winch. Only the cat's-paw held the rest of the anchor chain in its locker. He clung to a link of chain, and the *Caleche* slid sideways down the wave into the bottom of the trough and wallowed. With one hand on the great chain and one on the cat's-paw he waited for the swing of ship and

of anchor to balance gravity. The next wave rode in under
the ship, and she tilted now the other way. He wondered
dreamlike what the *Caleche*'s capsizing point was. She was
trying to climb a mountain sideways. The wave pushed farther beneath her, and she leaned farther away from it. The
anchor idly lifted, and tons of steel turned weightless. He
lifted the freed cat's-paw. Let the damned land thing tear
out it's locker. He wanted to get to his feet but was afraid
he would fall off the tilting, slippery deck. He held a deck
cleat and waited on his knees for her to right herself or turn
on her back. Riding before the crest of the waves she began
slowly to capsize. She passed the forty-five-degree angle,
picking up speed. He lay flat on his stomach now and
through the railing looked ten stories down into the green
valley. Then the crest of the wave passed, and he was looking into the side of the wave. Gravity pulled now the other
way. He rose to his feet, looked down the mile-long length
of wave, and heard the anchor chain running out.

But he couldn't make headway to the ladder. He couldn't
catch up to the ship's plunge down the wave. He crawled
on hands and knees as the bow swung down-wave, and
through the rain he saw the next great wave descending.
His knees jarred the deck as the bow cracked water and
submarined. Green sea lifted him and turned him end over
end. His center was lost. In green dimness he saw the anchor and its chain moving in a watery dream above him.
The chain tied itself into a simple knot and drifted away.
The water receded.

He lay wedged somewhere in a winch with both legs
twisted in metal and white bone glistening.

Rain splashed his open eyes and kept the white bones
cleansed of blood. Then water lifted him from the winch

and washed him against some housing. He thrashed his arms and his hand caught a line. He pulled for a door. Opening it, he tumbled inside onto a grating as heat from the engine room blew his face. Water poured in around him. From below came curses. A man ran across the engine room floor.

He dragged himself across the grating and across other gratings to the door marked Machine Shop. Inside, he locked the door and passed out with his face across his knees. He awoke dragging himself across the floor of the Machine Shop. One moment he was passed out, the next moment his fingers pulled at a seam. And he knew without thinking that he was pulling for the two pipes along the bulkhead. He let the ship roll him down against the pipes, then he wedged his foot between them and lay back. He held a stanchion and when the ship rolled away he released his hold. He hung by the broken leg. The white bone slid back into the stretched red flesh. Again he passed out, but that leg was set. And again he came awake pulling for the pipes. He wedged in the other foot and grabbed the stanchion of cool round steel. When the ship rolled away he shuddered and opened his fingers and hung by his other leg and passed out.

As if he had planned it all before, he opened his eyes and pulled down a can of heavy grease. He globbed a handful on each leg. Then he began seizing his legs with quarter-inch line. When he was finished, both legs were neatly seized from ankle to knee with ridged coils of line. He tied off and passed out again.

They had thought him washed over the side. It was the next day they found him wedged in between the table legs and the bulkhead. On his next trip to the Orient he had the tattoo man begin working on his fighting tattoos.

In the gloom of his room he looked at his outstretched legs. Now only he knew that beneath the smoking dragon and the snakes were the tattoos of butterflies and birds and flowers and pretty girls.

6

Delivered from the S.S. *Ekonk* to Dock 27 as follows:

Toilet paper. .4000 tons
Beer . . . . .2000 tons
Munitions . . . . .2000 tons
Caucasian flesh (frozen). . . . . 12 lbs.
Negroid flesh (frozen) . . . . .27 lbs.
Mongoloid flesh (frozen). . . . . .22 lbs.
Unidentified flesh (frozen). . . . . .12 lbs.
Assorted metals . . . . .116 lbs

> John L. Hammock
> Port Captain

Delivered from Dock 27 to the S.S.*Ekonk* as follows:

Coffins containing sandbags. 367
Coffins containing bodies or parts thereof . . .96
Stone artifacts. 16

> J. James James
> Captain, S.S. *Ekonk*

Chemistry

ON THE SIXTH DAY out of Long Song Bay the crew of the
S.S. *Ekonk* watched the sun go down and a night come without darkness. Some said the sun went down twice. Others
said the sun went down but came right back up again. The
Bosun told the Kid he'd heard this happened in these waters
every fifty years.

Just before the double day two submarines attacked the
Ekonk, but that part of it the Kid missed. The Bosun had
him busy learning hawser splicing. The Bosun had crooked
his finger at him, and he had followed the crooked finger up
and down ladders to their final descent into the empty forepeak. He and the Bosun were on their knees in the forepeak with a hawser snaked between them learning splicing
when the submarines attacked the convoy and the depth
charges exploded. The Kid was handing the splicing tools
to the Bosun while the Bosun explained their uses. With a
mallet the Bosun pounded a wooden fid between the hawser
strands. The fid's wooden point separated the strands, and
its fattening length widened the gap. "See the single fibers,"
the Bosun said. "By themselves they are not much. But

coiled together they are the hawser — the strongest line
aboard. All this strength from this weak fiber," the Bosun
said triumphantly.

The Kid bent to inspect a single brown fiber of hemp
when the deck jumped against his knees and the forepeak
walls gonged around them like a great drum.

The Kid was off his knees in a running crouch. "What
. . .?"

The Bosun missed one beat with the mallet.

"It is a depth charge," the Bosun said and swung the
mallet to the head of the fid.

The Kid aimed his crouch at the ladder and said, "A
what . . . ?"

"A depth charge," the Bosun said. "Hold the fid."

"A depth charge," the Kid repeated without realizing he
had spoken a word. He held the fid toward the ladder like
a baton.

"Hold it *here,*" the Bosun said pointing to the hawser.

"But, Boats . . ."

The Bosun's thick crusty hand guided the fid in his hand
to the hawser. "Steady now. Steady," said the Bosun.

He held the fid with his eyes on the ladder. His hand
jumped. He turned to see if the Bosun had hit his hand.
The forepeak gonged, and his head rang like a drum within
a drum. The Bosun's long gray hair waved like slow grass.

The Kid looked at the hawser, but he saw instead a torpedo explode and blow in one side of the forepeak. The
forepeak's steel plates exploded inward, and behind them
stood the crush of water.

There'd be no way out
Not with Boats
If he left now

Hit the ladder NOW
NOW

"I said, look," the Bosun said.

The tumbled gray head bent to the humped hawser. A thick finger with a split and blackened nail trembled as it traced the opening strands. "See how the fibers are undamaged by the wooden fid?" the Bosun asked. "It is slower than the metal spikes but better."

The Kid looked slack-jawed into the hole in the hawser, then at the Bosun. The Bosun's eyes were the color of seawater. The forepeak rang the Kid's head four times in quick succession.

"Jesus," he pleaded. "Let's get out of here."

The Bosun's head never raised. "We got this job to do, Kid."

So they knelt below the water line in the bottom of the empty forepeak splicing a hawser throughout the attack.

"Got what job?" the Kid asked.

"Splicing this hawser," the Bosun said pointing to the obvious.

"But it's only to teach me."

"They are all crazy out there," the Bosun said. "Hand me the mallet."

So he learned hawser splicing during the attack.

Finally the Bosun tied off the seizing and said, "Now." They climbed the ladder to stand at the railing on the bow. But what they saw were not submarines. The attack was over. Instead of submarines, they saw the sun go down and a night come without darkness.

"You will have to wait half a century to see this again," the Bosun said.

The ocean was filled with the wreckage of some past convoy. The black bow of a sunken freighter protruded from the water. Around the bow heaved torn bales of white cotton, pieces of brown wood, splintered boats, orange life jackets, bottles, buckets, cans — all, and the water, iridescent with what appeared to be oil. Each life jacket nested a black and swollen face to the sun. Then they saw that sometimes the blackened face was a black watch cap.

"What a stench," Red declared coming and leaning beside the Kid and the Bosun at the railing.

"Shouldn't we stop?" the Kid asked.

"The ship stops for the dead only to bury them," the Bosun said.

"Those are already in their graves," Red said. "What do you want to do? Haul them aboard, say something over them, and drop them back in the water? Hell, you want to say something, say it. Let's don't waste our own energy. Besides subs are maybe still around."

The Kid pointed a thin brown arm. "Look."

A dark flat mass flowed down the protruding bow of the sunken freighter and spread like a blanket over the water. It moved toward them. An overturned lifeboat floated in its flowing path. The flat mass slid over the lifeboat, blackened it, and flowed back onto the water.

"Hey," the Kid said, "those look like . . ."

"Rats!" the Bosun said.

"Rats?" Red asked.

"Those are rats," the Kid said.

The massed rats swam the swells for the *Ekonk's* side. The lead rat swam into the bow wave, its head high and sleek and black. Its claws scraped the *Ekonk's* plates. The other rats climbed over each other to claw at the passing ship. Their high hysterical cries filled the Kid's head like thunder. They climbed in mass up the ship's side, but the mass slid slowly aft and around the stern into the propeller. A few rats regrouped alongside the roiling wake and swam after the ship. The Kid and the Bosun and Red watched them disappear astern.

The Kid looked away from the rats and, so as not to look back at them, fastened his eyes to the huge pale sun sinking into the sea. "I'm on watch now," he said. "What do I watch for in all this?"

"Out," Red said tugging his skivvies up his bony hips.

"Out?" asked the Kid.

"Yes," the Bosun said. "You are the ship's eyes."

The Kid leaned into the v of the bow and watched the great sun set into the sea of garbage. He would watch for what he wanted. One thing certain: he would not watch the sea full of rats and death. He would watch the sky. The sun sank into the sea, and the western clouds turned sun-colored. The slowly heaving sea reflected the clouds. From the sun-colored water jutted cotton and men and broken ships. He watched the sun's colors fade from the clouds and the sky darken. But when the sky was dark the colors yet gleamed from the ocean. And the faces of Red and the Bosun glowed like full moons. On the bridge the Mate stepped through the glowing light to look into the water. The Mate's cap was pushed back and tilted.

"What's happening?" the Kid asked.

The sea glowed beneath a black sky.

Red lifted his hands, turning them in the glow. "Like day," he breathed.

The Bosun at the Kid's side in the v said, "Look!"

As far as the eye could see the ocean was luminous and golden. They sailed on sea-deep phosphorus, and the clinging phosphorus washed the ship's sides. The water line disappeared, and they sailed on light. They couldn't tell where the water and the ship joined. The white housing, the black stack, the straight masts, the bridge, and the focslehead on which they stood sailed not on water but on golden light.

"No," the Bosun said. "No, I mean look *there.*"

The Kid looked down into the sea. Luminous serpents with flat oval heads as broad as the hand swam the green-gold sea. The writhing creatures glowed even in the bright water. They writhed serpentine side by side, swaying together like dancers on the deep, and the Kid couldn't tell if they weaved in the water, or if the swells swung them, or both.

Then the Kid realized he was holding his breath. "I want to know what's happening," he said with alarm and fear. "What are those things?" And he heard a low growling beside him. Red, with closed eyes, dipped and swayed and growled tunefully. The Bosun's head was lowered and his hands raised.

Red with his arms curled overhead began swaying in time with the creatures. "Can you hear it?" he asked, cocking his head. "Can you hear it." He danced slowly among the gear on the focslehead.

Then Red's hands dropped to the railing beside the Kid, and he leaned far out. "I wonder how long they are," Red said matter-of-factly.

"If you had a big bucket," the Kid said. "But I'm out of it."

"Who's out of it?" the Bosun asked lifting his head as Red with a quick leap skipped down the focslehead ladder and disappeared.

The *Ekonk's* wake washed through the glowing oval heads and a life jacket nesting a dark face rode into the bow wave and disappeared. The face rode back out bobbing phosphorus hair and phosphorus eyes.

To the west golden clouds reappeared in the dark sky.

"The sun is rising back," the Kid said.

Red came skipping up the ladder. "Aha," he cried, shaking out an old newspaper. He tugged his skivvies and pranced the deck reading aloud the news by sealight.

The Bosun said to the Kid in the v, "When I was a boy, I saw this. Our Captain told us these things rise in this ocean every half a century, and he led us in prayer — *and dwell in the uttermost parts of the sea* — fifty years ago in this same light I was on a wooden deck on my knees" — *the night shineth as the day* —

"London," the prancing Red read. "The Alliance Countries and the Allied Countries have selected as the site . . ."

"I want to see better," the Kid said.

"You are not listening to me," the Bosun said. "Fifty years ago . . ." — *I was made in secret, and curiously wrought in the lowest parts of the earth* —

"Hey, Kid," Red called. "You want to see better you go look in a toilet bowl."

"Why?" the Kid asked.

"It's the place to get close to it all. Stop asking and go," Red said.

The Kid put a questioning face to the Bosun.

"If you won't listen to me," the Bosun said, "go on. You might learn it there."

A red blackout light faintly illumined the head. The two toilet bowls along that side of the wall flushed continuously and on the ceiling above each bowl wavered a golden circle.

The Kid stuck his head into the first circle. Seawater tumbled through the bowl like living fire. The Fat Fireman one day opened the door of the firebox to show him the power driving the ship through the water. Cautiously he stretched his hands to the water, but there was no heat. And more cautiously he dipped into the bright bowl. His hands came out dripping sparks from his fingers. He flipped his wrists and laughed as arcs of light flicked the dimness. Laughing, he splashed water onto the floor and shuffled in it. He stuck his thumbs in his ears and waggled glowworm fingers at the mirror on the opposite wall. Then he was before the mirror painting his face. He gilded his eyebrows, brightened his temples, smudged on a sparkling mustache and mouth, tinted his cheeks. Then gazing ever more solemnly, he watched the lights go out on his face.

To get back the laughter he dipped into the bowl again and flicked his fingers, but it occurred to him that when the arcing lights disappeared in midair, something died. He bent to the bowl and splashed his arms to the elbow. With gold bending each hair, he left the head with outstretched hands.

The Satchel Man stood outside in the companionway with his head in his hands. The Satchel Man hung against the bulkhead from the palms of his own two hands. His left jaw bulged the size of half an orange. "Toothache," he mumbled backing away from the Kid's arms.

"They were alive," the Kid said as the lights on the hairs began to dim.

The Satchel Man nodded, eyes aching dully in their caves. "Phosphorus."

"Little animals," the Kid said. "I guess when they go out they die."

"Phosphorus," repeated the Satchel Man through clenched teeth. "Chemistry."

"No, live things."

"So's my jaw full," the Satchel Man muttered.

"But these only rise every fifty years. The Bosun told me."

"Depth charges," the Satchel Man said. "The depth charges brought them up."

Then dry lids closed over the Satchel Man's eyes. He hung from his two hands and behind the closed lids the Kid could see the eyes moving, looking in all directions. The hands raised the hollow face, and the eyelids raised. "Help me."

"Sure," the Kid said. "Sure — "

The hands turned the head and carried the Satchel Man away.

The Satchel Man swung down the companionway.

"Wait," the Kid called.

He watched the Satchel Man tilt away between the walls. Then in an optic leap he saw it was not the Satchel Man who tilted, but the ship. The Satchel Man swung exactly down the center of the companionway, unaffected by the ship's gentle rolls. And the Kid saw how the older sailors did it, how they could walk so straight. The Satchel Man ignored the ship. Like the creatures outside he was walking the waves. The Satchel Man's feet were as inseparable from the waves as were the waves from the tides and the tides from the earth.

Emerging again into the light on deck the Kid tried to walk a long, straight deck weld. With arms outstretched, swaying, trying to forget the ship, he still found it like walking a railroad track atop a moving train. Head erect, he paced the focslehead in the light, trying to ignore the ship, until he stumbled over a cleat and almost over the side.

"Now what the hell are you doing?" Gene asked as they were going aft after the watch was over.

"Walking this deck weld."

"What?"

"Walking this weld."

"Weld? Why don't you hop up on the railing? Jesus! Here we are in the middle of an ocean with light coming up instead of down, we got day instead of night, and you're taking a drunk test."

"But I can't do it," the Kid said. "I can't anticipate the way the Satchel Man can. That means he's wrong when he says it's chemistry."

Gene stopped his slide halfway down a ladder. "The Satchel Man walks welds?"

Coming down the ladder behind him, the Kid couldn't stop his skipping feet. "It means he had to learn it," he said sliding onto Gene's back. "He didn't get born knowing what waves are doing. You do it, and I bet you don't even know it."

"Hell, Kid," Gene said untangling himself, "I don't even know what we're talking about."

"About walking to where you want to go when everything around is moving."

"What?"

"He said it was chemistry, but chemistry doesn't make you able to walk the sea. Chemistry didn't make my mother wash or iron or tie shoelaces. Monday she washed, Tuesday she ironed, Wednesday she baked, and she tied shoelaces even after I was grown sometimes. Chemistry may bring up those things in the water every half a century, or depth charges, but it doesn't make Monday washday, or tie a grown boy's shoes. She did it because she *wanted* to do it. She chose it. And chemistry doesn't make your feet know waves either."

In the shower stalls they sluiced hot water down their backs while the circles glowed on the ceiling. As they toweled, the Kid looked into the near bowl, his face aglow and his shadow dark on the ceiling.

Gene's head made a second shadow. "You think that's really something, huh, Kid? You wait'll we get to Joetown."

"Why?"

"There's real life there."

"More'n this?"

"Dumb Kid. People life. Women. Beer and women. Our life. Not this shit."

As they climbed into their bunks, the Satchel Man turned in his bunk and moaned.

"You'll love it," Gene whispered across the dark.

In his bunk the Satchel Man steered an imaginary ship through an imaginary sea. He was trying to forget the bloody strip of towel clenched in the hole in his jaw. When he got the imaginary waves high enough, he could forget anything. But these lapping four-foot waves didn't use the first part of his mind. What he needed were fifty-footers tossing the bow forty-five degrees in the blink of an eye. The big ones he steered straight into sleep. These four-footers didn't even get Gus's knee out of his chest.

Gus had braced his knee against his rib cage, and behind the chair Blackie held his forehead in laced fingers.

"Got him?" Gus asked.

"Got him," Blackie said. And his head was pulled back into Blackie's hard belly.

Gus stuck the cold slightly greasy pliers into his mouth then pulled them back out. "You sure you want me to get all three?"

He spat over the arm of the chair. "I can't tell which one by tapping."

"Three," Gus said and stuck the cold pliers back in again.

If they had been lowers, Gus would have pulled his jaw off.

He steered through the four-footers without trying.

The hurting in his head was only nerves sending signals to each other. Just chemistry. A door slammed and slammed in his head. But everything was chemistry. His chemistry had made the sperm. Her chemistry had made the egg. The egg and the sperm had made an independent chemistry to buck and kick in his arms. Starfish hands touched and measured and pulled his nose. In her sleep with all her miniature organs busy and her pulse mouth open, a roar of life hung around her little body. He heard it.

He heard it as his wife's stomach grew. Lying beside his wife in bed, he pulled the magazine from her face.

But I'm reading

It's a girl

What?

She's a girl, and she's making her hands in there

What? You what? as the magazine slid to the floor

I know what she's doing in there, making hands, she's a dynamo

Are you dreaming?

In front of the stoplight, on Fourth Street, while he sat in the car waiting in the five o'clock traffic, she began making her liver.

He moaned.

Underneath the pine trees in the park he stopped the swing, and his hands fumbled together the tiny buttons on her red coat. He looked into her blue eyes and saw his own reflection. She reached cold hands to his cheeks. *I see me in your eyes,* she said.

He moaned.

The front door closed to the width of his wife's disapproving face. And peering out from beneath her face, down around her knees, one tiny blue eye watched him from the narrowing gap.

He moaned.

They were still four-footers.

Chemistry.

He knelt beside the empty crib and shook the vacant bars. He held the crib's emptiness in his two hands and shook it. The nerves pumped his head to bursting, and the front door slammed and slammed and slammed. Waves slammed and slammed the ship's side, great quartering waves fifty feet high. He buried his head in the binnacle and drove the needle by the card.

"You'll really love it," Gene whispered again in the dark.

"I hope so," the Kid whispered back. "I want it."

Joetown

1

Two days from Joetown the Captain in his cabin quit drinking. Normal voices got louder. A round-the-clock poker game started in the messroom. Peewee hung a white suit to sun on the well deck. Shoes were taken from lockers, shined, and restowed. And the Satchel Man quit reading in his bunk and lay staring at the springs above.

The Kid saw the land first, and all afternoon he watched it grow, a whole continent of land. The Bosun had the deck crew out preparing the ship for cargo handling. As they topped the booms, worked the hatches, unlashed the gangway, one would now and then stand with work in hand gazing landward. Red was on a hatch knocking out wedges with a sledgehammer when he lowered the hammer and hitched his sagging skivvies with the leather cuffs of his gloves. Looking landward over their heads, he said, "I don't know where we're going, but when we get there somebody's going to get it."

Gene pointed. "There's the river."

A brown highway thrust through the ocean from the green-black land. They sailed alongside the reach of river, and the brown water darkened. The distance between the *Ekonk* and the side of the darkening river never varied.

"Who's at the wheel?" Gus asked.

"The Satchel Man, who else can steer so straight," Red said hopping off the hatch.

And that's when the Bosun signaled the last boom topped and turned to the Kid fastening a line to a cleat. "Kid, you will stand gangway watch tonight."

"*Me.* Why me?" The Kid jerked at the line. "I want to go ashore. Do you know how long . . .?"

"We all know how long," the Bosun said, for the first time not giving the Kid's work a studied look but only including it in the final glance around the whole deck. "You'll get there soon enough. Won't hurt you to keep from trouble one more day."

"But hell . . .!"

Gene gave the Kid a slap on the back that angered him. "Don't worry, Kid. What's there's been there a long time. It won't go away."

"But . . ."

The Satchel Man eased the *Ekonk* into the river mouth among the other ships. They dropped anchor to wait their turn for the fifty river miles into the jungle for ore. Then they trooped to the Captain's cabin to draw shore money, all except the Satchel Man. He went to lie in his bunk, and while the others showered and dressed, the Kid lay in his bunk.

"Wait'll you see the Ice Chest," Red said to Gus. "Every room has a toilet and basin and big bathtub all inlaid with red roses, beautiful!"

"I've seen it," Gus said buttoning a Hawaiian shirt.

Red turned to Blackie. "Can you imagine pissing in a bed of roses? Built by this guy went into the jungle and come out with his pockets full of diamonds. Built him this dream whorehouse, open air, up high, on stilts to get away from the mosquitoes and catch the air. Said he never wanted to be hot again. Under it is this ice house . . ."

"Red, you'd believe anything," Gene said.

"You think that's not true," Red said following Gene out on deck. "Him and me were shipmates. I was with him the night he jumped ship. Wanted me to go with him. But . . ." Red said spreading his palms, "I was married then."

"You," Gene said, "How old do you think you are?"

Red's lids hooded. "I could of changed your old man's diapers."

"Hell, Red, you might be my old man." Gene in a creased white shirt and with rings bristling from each middle finger hitched his thick belt and tugged at his black watch cap. "Did you by any chance hit Galveston around nineteen and —"

"Man I know," Gus said in an unemotional voice, "if he can't fight with gloves, uses rings."

At the head of the gangway Gene turned his hands showing the rings. "For the ladies," he smiled.

"Hah!" Gus cried, fishing a cigarette from his shirt. "Half a pound of fighting iron on each hand to handle women. You come at me with those I'll stuff your balls through them."

Gene tapped his stomach with the heel of his fist. "First sign of trouble I suck those jiggers up this iron gut. But if a man's got the need to try . . ."

"Man I want to try," Blackie said, "is that Chief Mate."

Sliding his six-inch steps the Bosun came to the gangway in a new khaki shirt and breeches and slicked hair.

Peewee, fingering his mustache, told the Fat Fireman, "Soak this in cold beer it grows an inch a day and curls like a water spout." Peewee wore a narrow white hat, white shoes, white shirt, white suit, and a tongue of yellow flame for a tie. The Fat Fireman was the only other crewman wearing a suit. In it he looked strong instead of fat.

The skinny oarsman, black as the *Ekonk*'s side, slid his bumboat beneath the gangway, and the Captain came down the deck in a brown business suit carrying a small bag and talking to one of the mates and a shriveled engineer. They too carried small bags, as did the Cook coming from the galley in his sharkskin suit and Panama hat.

"You don't mind if we go first," the Captain asked, motioning the Engineer down the gangway. "The boat looks large enough, Cook. Would you join us? And McIlhenny? And you, Hildebrandt?"

The Fat Fireman and Peewee followed the Cook down the gangway.

As the bumboat bobbed away from the *Ekonk*'s side with everybody sitting stiff-backed and holding on, Blackie said, "*McIlhenny? Hildebrandt?*"

"Which one's which," asked the Kid.

"Don't make any difference," Gus said. "Give the Fat Fireman all the names in the world he's still the Fat Fireman. And you — you're the Kid."

"The Captain mostly knows shore names," the Bosun said, motioning the others down the gangway. "Kid, you will take a turn on the deck on the hour."

"And listen for the drunks coming back," Gene called. "Some of these others may need help."

"Ha!" Gus said.

Then the second bumboat bobbed away with everyone like sticks and holding on.

The Kid.

He went to the messroom for coffee. *Shore names.* The only names he really knew were Gene and Gus, and they were first names. Back home he sometimes didn't know a first name, but he always knew last names. He never had sorted out all those Harris cousins, but whichever one it was he and everybody else in the countryside knew it was a Harris.

These were working names. Everybody'd known everybody two days at sea.

I'm Gene

Gus

How many crews had looked into their daring faces and remembered?

And he was the Kid.

He had stepped across the gangway, and the Kid was born weighing a hundred and forty pounds. Except that wasn't right. It had taken more than crossing the gangway. He had needed to be new, and all new ones weren't called the Kid. Gene looked at him over the rim of a smoking cup of coffee one morning and said, "Last ship I was on we had this new-assed punk from Newark. To give him credit he was smart enough to jump ship first port we hit."

Imagine things being so bad he'd leave the *Ekonk* here in Joetown. He toured the deck checking the anchor lights and all the floodlights, and he measured the distant shore to see if the *Ekonk* was dragging anchor. Joetown's lights marked the edge of a broad river. They streaked to his feet, and music beat the water and wavered on the wind. He leaned over the bow railing thinking he saw a phosphorus movement in the water. But this water came from the jun-

gle. On the map the river looked to drain half a continent.
The creek past his home drained half a mountain. This
black river came out the side of a continent; the creek came
out the side of the mountain. The creek was the sweetest
water he ever tasted, full of minerals and the mountain.

You like that? his father asked from a dripping face.

They were spraddled on the rock ledge sucking at the
creek where it broke from the mountain.

I like it

It's the mountain's waste fluids, his father said.

He thought on that with the seashells in his pocket. And
when he fished or swam or drank the water, he fished and
swam and drank the sap of fallen trees and fallen animals
and fallen rain that soaked through the mountain's rock as
through a sponge.

From the ledge he brought the spring water home in
earthen jars and hung them to cool in their own evapora-
tion. And when the water shaped to his mouth, he wondered at the shapes he held.

"I swear," his mother said, "he'd rather drink that water
than eat."

"It's sweet water," his father said. And whenever his father felt sick he always believed he'd have a glass of the
boy's mountain. And on hot days when her work sweated
her, his mother believed she'd have a cool drink too.

He wondered at the shapes held beneath the river's flat,
dark surface. Shapes he could only dream about.

Alan Truesdale killed a panther on the other side of the
mountain once. It was the last ever seen around there.
Gene told him they mined every kind of ore in the jungle
here and crystals of every color. That meant he floated on
gold and silver and diamonds.

The surface of the water heaved, and again he thought he saw something. But again it was gone.

He made another tour of the decks, checking lights and checking the anchor. The tide was going out now, and combined with the flow of the river, the dark water moved to sea at better than eight knots. The creak of oarlocks crossed the water and talk and curses. Around midnight the oarlocks creaked to the *Ekonk's* side and the Bosun transferred from the bobbing bumboat to the gangway with slow care. He climbed into the floodlight, one foot up both feet on. He stopped, swayed, then pulled hard on the chain railing. The Kid reached down to help him the last two gangway steps. The Bosun jerked away.

"No," he mumbled.

On deck the Bosun stood head down and resting, mumbling, "No." He was very drunk.

The Bosun moved out of the gangway light, keeping one hand always on the railing, and he followed at a distance. The Bosun passed the dim figure of the Satchel Man sitting on a hatch and paused. They looked at each other wordlessly. Then the Bosun went on, and after a moment, the Satchel Man followed him into the focsle.

In a few moments the Satchel Man reappeared to sit beside the Kid on the hatch.

"He's in his bunk now. The others will be coming aboard soon . . ."

"He wanted no help from me," the Kid said. "And why didn't he put you on gangway watch? Didn't he know you weren't going ashore?"

"He knows I never go ashore in foreign ports," the Satchel Man said.

"Never?"

The Satchel Man turned toward him in the night and after a while said, "He wanted the crew to blow off a little steam before you went with them. Tonight they'll fight even if they have to fight among themselves."

"I can take care of myself," the Kid said wondering if he could. One slip on the gangway and the Bosun's body would be a mile at sea by now.

"The Bosun is having his last shore leave," the Satchel Man said. "They only hired him for one trip. After this it's no money, no job, nothing but years and sea knowledge. But do you know what? He's luckier than most. He can go ashore now."

The Kid waited, but the quiet voice remained silent.

"Wish I could," the Kid said.

"You will, and I will when there's somebody to go to. I wait'll the trip's over. We get back to the States, I get my money and head for a bar I know. I know one every port. If I can get to it before I start drinking, I give the man that runs it my payoff. He keeps me drunk, gets me registered at the Union Hall. I sleep in back, and when my money's gone, he ships me out again, and I wake up two days at sea."

"Are they honest?"

"Not the way you're thinking, but they get me back to sea. It's the only way I can make it ashore. But the Bosun'll get along now that he's old. You know the one other place I can keep it going ashore?"

"Where?"

"Jail. You know something else, Kid?"

"What?"

"You're not a sailor. This is all make-believe to you. Old Boats has picked the wrong guy to teach."

"I've been planning this since I was a boy," the Kid protested.

The Satchel Man lay back on his elbows and looked at the stars.

"That's why you're different. You planned it. The Bosun's teaching you one thing, you're learning another. It's all right," the Satchel Man said as the Kid started to protest again. "It's all right. You'll go home in a trip or two, and you'll remember us and these days, and they'll be good memories, I know because I've watched you sleep. But while you're remembering, remember that we'll still be out here. Remember *that* while you're remembering."

The Kid turned toward the Satchel Man knowing as his head turned that he was right, that he had never imagined himself an old man at sea for the simple reason he'd never thought that far ahead. At sea he was the Kid.

"Yessir," he said.

"Don't wait too long to go back," the Satchel Man said, "or you'll be going to sea without planning it."

"How did you know before I did?"

"We all know it, even the Bosun. He teaches you and the crew accepts you because you believe you're one of us."

"What about when I was on that crosstree? I wouldn't have gone if I hadn't been a sailor."

"You went because you believed you were. You believe in things. We *are*. You're from what is called good folks, as I once was, and I don't mean that so much as a compliment as that you believe in things. If you really wanted to go ashore tonight you'd go. The Bosun said you were on gangway watch, so you believed it."

"But I am," the Kid insisted.

"You put yourself on it. Those guys we saw bombed on that mountaintop put themselves there too."

"Yessir," the Kid said.

"Listen to you. The dirty drunk you bathed is now *sir*. You're a real believer. Just remember what I told you, Kid. It's all chemistry." The Satchel Man was now standing on deck stretching.

"But that's a belief, too," the Kid said.

The Satchel Man cocked his head at him.

"Guess I'll sleep out tonight," the Satchel Man said after a moment. "Focsle will be a little noisy. And when they come aboard don't you get any ideas because you're on watch you should interfere. And, Kid — "

"Yessir."

"There's no belief in chemistry. It is."

The Satchel Man walked into semidarkness. He reappeared stepping into a floodlit companionway amidships.

The Kid was touring the deck when he heard the oarlocks coming. He heard no voices until Slim the Oiler charged up the gangway and hopped on deck. "Send him up," Slim shouted. "Send the punk up." Slim clenched and unclenched his fists and couldn't keep his feet still.

Blackie's white face appeared over the railing. His head lolled on a neck as limber as a loose string. "What's the matter with you guys? Huh? Hey c'mon now." He wobbled a grin at Slim, friendly and pleading. His arm waved in front of him. "Hey, Kid, what's matter with these guys, can't take a little — "

Slim knocked his arm aside and decked him.

Blackie lay on his side cursing and pushing at the deck. The Kid leaned down to help him as the rest of the bumboat load came aboard. They came kicking. The first foot hit Blackie's straightening arms and rolled him down again.

"Hey now —"

The second sank to the instep in Blackie's stomach.

A knee caught the Kid's ribs knocking him back against the housing. Booted feet flew around his head. Set white faces hung above the kicking feet.

"Let me at him," Peewee cried kicking the kicking legs. Peewee's yellow tie was missing; his shirt flapped loose, torn in back from collar to tail.

"Let me!"

Rolling along the deck Blackie cursed and tried to gain his feet. They kicked him back down and crowded the narrow deck walk to get at him. Gene and Gus brought up the rear. Gene was laughing.

The Kid got to his feet in time to see Blackie spill backward down a ladder, arms and legs flying in every direction. On the next deck Blackie stumbled to his feet in a weaving crouch. "Come on!" he cried, "The more you kick my iron balls the shinier they get. Come on, all of you!"

They did.

They kicked him down and booted him along the deck. He tucked into a ball and held himself in his arms. His cursing stopped. They rolled him the length of the deck to the focsle entrance, and he stuck there against the foot-high coaming until he raised himself to a white shoe that spilled him inside. They piled in after him and booted him to his bunk and beneath it where he lay curled and still.

"Bastard deserved it," Peewee cried.

"He's a punk," the Fat Fireman said.

They backed away, spent.

The Fat Fireman crawled into his bunk clothes and all and began to snore. Some undressed. The Kid knelt be-

side Blackie's bunk. Blackie's breath was labored. He lay
with closed eyes, one arm twisted beneath him. The Kid
wanted to pull his arm free, but he was afraid to help him,
afraid even to show sympathy. They might turn on him.
He was on their side.

"What did he do?" he asked again.

Gene and Gus were looking at each other across the
empty middle of the focsle.

"What did he do?" he asked again.

Gene looked briefly toward him, then back to Gus. They
both walked out on deck with the Kid following. They
stopped about ten feet apart facing each other. The Kid
started to ask again, but seeing their faces he backed down
the deck. He was not a part of this.

Gus's head hung forward. "Well?" he asked.

"Yes," Gene said sounding tired. "Of course."

"Well, come on," Gus said.

"Gus, you're bound and determined to have a piece of me
this trip, at least try." Gene stripped the rings from his fingers. Then he laughed. He turned full circle and laughed
and shook his head. "Gus, why are we doing this?"

Gus looked at his balled hands. "We're going to see who's
the winner, who can take it and who can dish it out.
Besides, what else is there to do?"

"Nothing, I guess," Gene said. "I guess nothing."

They moved toward each other, and the Kid in terror
stumbled at a ladder and stood alone in the gangway light.
He could never be a part of this.

Once he peeked around the edge of the housing. Gene
and Gus rolled together on the floodlit deck locked in each
other's arms. He went back to the gangway light.

On his next tour of deck Gene and Gus were gone from

beneath the floodlight. Gus's shirt lay torn on the deck. Gene lay on the canvas-covered hatch on his back. Gene was talking to himself, whispering his name over and over.

Gene

Gene

I'm Gene

"Are you all right, Gene?" the Kid called as though afraid of waking him.

Gene's voice stopped. He tried to raise himself but fell back. His hands were swollen into fists, and his nose was split like an overripe fruit.

"I'm sleeping out tonight," Gene said.

The Kid went away in the dark and brought a wet towel that he placed wordlessly beside Gene's swollen hand. Gene covered his face with it and moaned.

On the bow the Kid checked the *Ekonk* against the shore lights. In the lights he saw clearly a movement in the water. A giant ray was circling the ship. He followed as it slid barely beneath the surface with no apparent effort. Moving past the ray to the stern he waited with a thick plank balanced on the railing.

He dropped the plank end first on the ray's back. Startled flukes thrust the water, and the great ray was gone seaward leaving the *Ekonk* rocking gently in its wake.

What could Blackie have done to them? He did not believe in this any longer.

Sitting between Gus and Gene in the Ice Chest, the Kid learned that Blackie had not *done* anything. But he could hardly believe it. Gus's eyes were slits, and Gene's eyes above the nose tape were yellow turning purple. They were watching the women at the bar.

"Forget it," Gene told the Kid. "He's just — "

"He's a punk," Gus interrupted.

Ignoring the interruption, Gene handed Gus the salt.

"Thanks," Gus said pouring some in his hand.

Gene laughed. "You're welcome, sir, you bastard, don't you have any connection between your jaw and brain?"

"None you'll ever find," Gus said matter-of-factly. "But I been knocked out."

He had not meant to come ashore with Gene or Gus or with any of them. When they left the long walkway connecting the bumboat platform to the shore, the rest of the crew went one way, he went another. He had avoided them all during the day. The Bosun hadn't seemed to care what any of them did so long as they looked busy when he left his jar of tea and rum on the messroom table and toured the deck. Gene with his nose taped together spent the day in the shade of a lifeboat painting its bottom. Gus chipped paint all day with an automatic hammer. He set the dull-nosed hammer pounding the steel deck and set his swollen face. No one neared his wall of noise.

He painted.

He rigged a sling and pulley and dropped himself over the side, and, dangling his feet above the rush of dark water, he blackened the *Ekonk*'s plates. When he climbed back on deck at coffee time, they razzed him about what waited for him ashore, but he said he wasn't going ashore with them, he was going to a movie or a drugstore or something. And when he stepped off the swaying wooden walkway onto the solid ground, he stood with his feet spread waiting to see the direction they took. He went the other way.

"Hey, Kid," Gene called. "It's the same everywhere. Don't fight it."

His feet jarred the ground, and he found Joetown two blocks deep. The first block was bars and cafes, the second small dark shops. Immediately he had a following of little boys with shoeshine boxes.

"Shine, Meester?"

He shook his head. Music was everywhere. Every bar, every cafe had its own jukebox.

"You want fuckee?"

He shook his head and crossed a half-dirt half-stone street to get rid of them. He crossed back and forth between the two blocks and found the blocks always the same. Bright-mouthed women with dark faces sat in the bars and cafes looking toward the street. In the dark streets he passed only men. The shine boys picked them up in the corner streetlights and gave them up at the next.

"Fuckee, Meester?"

He shook his head. At the end of the next street there was no streetlight. The wooden buildings with balconies stopped. The road went off into the darkness. He retraced his steps.

"Shine, Meester?"

"Fuckee?"

"Give me money?"

He shook his head back past the walkway to the bumboat landing, turned two corners, and there was the Ice Chest as Red had described it: on stilts, taller than the other buildings, bigger, with the heavy doors of an ice house on the ground floor, and on the second floor Gene leaned an arm on a peeled log railing. Across the street beneath the street-light a shine rag snapped music against the Bosun's shoe. The Bosun had one foot on the shine box and his hands on the steadying heads of two shine boys. The Bosun waggled hello off the top of a head. He waved and climbed the split log steps into the Ice Chest.

The *Ekonk* crew were scattered around tables on the far side of the room. "Over here," Blackie called, pointing to an empty chair next to Red. He waved but crossed to Gene's table and sat between Gene and Gus.

"What'd I tell you," Gene said. "Why fight it?"

"They don't have any movies or drugstores in this place," the Kid explained.

Gus waved his arm and ordered a round of drinks for the *Ekonk* tables. Other crews sat at other tables. The room was not so much a room as a second floor without walls. Log pillars and the railing encircled the room. The third floor was a series of doors behind an inner balcony. A woman in green satin walked along the balcony and down a stairway at the end of a long bar. From the bar stools women in electric dresses watched the room with painted faces. Before them was a dance floor.

The Kid had half finished his beer when the waiter put another round on the table. He lined it behind the first. "But what did Blackie do?" he asked.

"It's not what he does, it's what he is," Gene said. "And you worry too much. Look at that one."

She was in red. Her hips snapped as she weaved in front of a sailor in his twenties who lifted one foot then the other and held on. When the music stopped, the young sailor took her back to his table.

"Too early for that," Gene said. "She'll *drink* his money."

He drank faster, but now three beers were lined before him. The bolder sailors went to the bar and talked to the women. The boldest danced.

"Talk about a busman's holiday," Gene said rising. He

hitched his belt over to a woman in a lavender dress and dyed red hair. Gus grunted, and the Kid rubbed the back of his hand across his lips. They felt blue and numb.

"Here," Red said, thrusting a glass at him "Try this."

He protested, but Red insisted. "Come on. You'll like it."

It tasted of lemons, and he did like it.

"See."

"Excuse me. I've got to go to the head." He walked past the bar through the heavy perfume and tried not to look. Most of them showed a lot of crossed leg. The one with Gene called, "Hey, Kid," and kicked her foot at him. He nodded hello and smiled. Then someone had his arm at the elbow, and he came to a turning stop. He turned to a halt facing a boy his own age. The other Kid had a black watch cap pushed back on his head too and was saying something in a funny voice. They were the same height, but muscular, sun-darkened arms hung from the other Kid's short-sleeved red shirt. He wore baggy breeches and the brightest red socks he'd ever seen.

"What did you say?" he asked through numbed lips.

The other Kid smiled and tugged his elbow to a table where he made introductions in the funny voice. The others rose and shook his hand, and someone handed him a glass of beer. He and the other Kid sat facing, his eyes blue, the other Kid's yellowed and murky. Over the rim of his glass he asked the other Kid where he was from. The other Kid smiled and raised his glass.

"I'm from Arkansas," he said. "That's in the United States."

The other Kid smiled and raised his glass.

He looked to the others. Across the table a dark-eyed man with graying hair scowled at him. When their eyes met, the man's mouth smiled, but the rest of his face stayed the same.

Gus

Hell, he could talk to horses and chickens and cows and dogs, surely he could talk to a different human.

He stuck his index finger in his own chest, then he said slowly and distinctly as to a child, "Me from Ark and saw."

The other Kid laughed, shook his head, and clicked their glasses.

How in the hell did the crews manage to get in fights if they couldn't argue. "We have to use another kind of language," he said smiling and raising his glass: Click. They took turns clicking their glasses in silent toasts until his glass was empty. Getting to his feet, he touched the other Kid's corded arm. The other Kid got to his feet and patted his shoulder. They both laughed. Then everybody at the table laughed, and he went on to the head.

Sure enough the toilet bowl was full of roses. It was the first public toilet he'd ever seen with a bathtub, a huge one that was a mass of twining roses the same red as those on his mother's back trellis.

Back at his table red-dyed hair hung over the back of his chair. Scraping up another chair his knee brushed her thigh, which gave like a balloon. She smiled at him and Gene lifted the long red hair and whispered into it. Her smile broadened. She turned full toward him, searching his face with curiosity.

"Cherry?" she said laughing.

"What?" he asked. He couldn't believe she meant what he thought she did.

"Hey, Gus, he's blushing," Gene said.

"Hell, no, I'm not blushing, I mean, hell no, I'm no cherry."

She patted his cheek as he jerked away. She might as well have chucked him under the chin.

"He's sweet, I like him."

She rose swinging her hair and leaned her breasts around his head.

Even Gus laughed at his face.

As she crossed to the bar he stacked his beers on a nearby table.

"Hey," Gene laughed, "he's taking his beers and going off alone."

He lined them on the table and was insulted. She was so soft she frightened him, a full-grown woman, and the sailors were taking them back to their tables now. How did they do it with all the different languages? Gene said only a few of the women spoke English. His eyes caught the other Kid's and they waved. Each crew had a boundary, and his crew had inner boundaries. Did the crews just walk over and start pounding each other?

The woman swung her red hair up the stairs and down the balcony with the woman in green. They came back with a slender woman in yellow. The one in yellow, swaying to the music, leaned over the balcony railing. The Kid at the other table waved to her and she waved back, but her eyes were searching. Looking around the room, her eyes met his and passed through him cool and light as wind. And now the painted faces of the women at the bar were looking at him.

"Hey, Kid," Gene called, "your cherry's got the girls all shaking their tails and twittering. Hey you guys, you'll get your money's worth here tonight. Everybody here'll get a piece of the Kid."

"Hell," the Kid said, "just you Hell."

The woman in yellow descended the stairs. Stopping at

the jukebox she looked into its colored machinery and danced standing still in a way he had never seen. Then she looked behind the jukebox and shook her head. She began dancing again, oblivious to the room, standing still and making the same movements over and over until the woman in green stopped her and pointed at him. She came across the dance floor *straight for his table.*

She pulled out a chair beside him and sat down with her thick black hair falling around coppery almost black skin. Her eyes were as blue as the sea. She wore no makeup. She took a beer in long dark-nailed fingers and looked directly into his eyes. *Why she was younger than he was.*

He nodded.

She nodded, and they both looked away at the same time.

He felt the heat of her across the table, or maybe the heat of her presence. His skin tingled, and his stomach turned weak. Crossing her legs she touched his foot, and he jerked back bumping his knee under the table.

"What's your name?" he asked.

Her shoulders lifted in a shrug.

"Don't you speak English either?"

Her blue eyes looked at him through the falling black hair. "Fuckee." she whispered.

"Gene!"

Gene and Red Hair came over.

"Doesn't she speak English?"

"Kid," Gene said. "Red says she came downriver in a dugout three days ago. She's from some tribe in the interior and an old geezer down the street is the only guy in town can talk her lingo. She's got a goddamned shamrock around her neck hammered out of solid gold. Says it's her magic and she's on her way to Ireland to find her father's spirit.

Hell, Kid, a week ago she was running the jungle naked, and now you know it all except for — "

Red Hair put a hand over Gene's mouth and said, "Shh, let her show him."

He rubbed the back of his hand across his numbed lips as Red Hair pulled him erect by the arm. Motioning the girl to her feet too, she pointed at him, then upstairs.

The girl took his hand, and he grabbed for his beers and got two. She led him across the dance floor to the stairs. He followed like a tethered old animal. It was a long way across the smooth boards. Then the other Kid was in front of them barring the way up the stairs. He saluted with his beer only to have the other Kid knock it high in the air. From his other side the scowling man shoved him toward the street stairs. He looked down into the darkness of the stairwell and was as frightened as he had ever been in his life. Hands shoved him again. Down there they would have him alone. Separated. He tried to think of a solution to the darkness.

Then the beer hit the dance floor with a dull slosh, and Gene was beside him with a bottle in his fist. "Goddamn you, you touch the Kid and I'll kick the shit out of you and every other Greek in the joint." The scowling man stopped the other Kid with an outstretched hand. He looked Gene over carefully, looked at his bottle, at his rings, then he turned the other way and looked into Gus's swollen smiling face.

The scowling man pushed the other Kid back to their table.

"Go on," Gene told him, and he found he still held her hand. She pointed a long finger at the bar, leaned against him, and whispered, "Fuckee?"

He showed her his other beer and pulled her up the

stairs. She followed reluctantly, until with another shrug she took the lead and he followed her along the balcony rail. She stopped before one of the doors, and as the door closed behind them he realized it closed the whistles and cheers of the *Ekonk* crew.

The room held a bed, a chair, and a naked baby in a wooden box stamped AMPONIC TOOLS. The box was on the floor before an open-shuttered window overlooking the river, and she was on her knees beside it cooing and freeing her breasts from the yellow dress. He stood uncertainly while she sat cross-legged on the floor nursing the bobbing head.

Someone rapped at the door, but she paid no attention so he opened it onto the woman in green who babbled at him in a language he couldn't understand.

"We could click glasses," he said. "If we had glasses."

She babbled and shook her head and held out her hand. He took out his money, and she took some of the bills, then she took some more, but before she could get more, he stuffed the money back in his pocket.

He locked the door, pulled up the one chair, and sat with his guts and throat strung together in an ache while the baby nursed. Once he stretched his fingers to her hair but didn't touch it. When the baby finished, she turned bare-breasted and held the naked little boy before him. He touched its cheek. She put the now sleeping baby back in his box and turned to him still on her knees.

She shook back the black hair and pointed into her mouth. "Fuckee," she said.

"What?"

Pointing into her mouth, she said urgently, "Fuckee. Fuckee." She began making chewing motions.

He too began making chewing motions and pointing into

his mouth saying, "Fuckee." Then he stopped. "Food," he said. "You mean food. Not the other. You got it all fucked up."

He went to the bar and the bartender said, "She only eats fried egg sandwiches." He bought three.

While she ate the sandwiches with her back to him, he drank beer looking beyond the baby and out the window to the lights of the ships on the river. One was the *Ekonk*. His home. He was from Arkansas, and he'd seen a man kicked half the length of a ship. They gave it to Blackie, but they came to his help. And he didn't even like Gus. With a start he realized he wouldn't have done the same for Gus, maybe not for any of them. Maybe he *was* different. There could have been guns or knives or anything. But Gene didn't think of that, he acted. And Gus —

Her long dark fingers nudged his knee. She smiled, chewing the last of the second sandwich. The third she hid in the bathroom. In the brief light the tangled roses twined the bathroom in wild growth.

When she stepped back through the bathroom door into the semidark room, she left her yellow dress on the floor. Her long coppery body gleamed in the half-light and her eyes peered sea-blue from beneath the black hair. The golden shamrock gleamed above her breasts. She began to make clucking noises deep in her throat and to dance the same movement over and over without moving her feet, until at last he realized the dance was bringing her slowly toward him.

He stood from the chair in an ache, wondering if his knees would hold. And he couldn't raise his arms. Not until she slowly weaved against him.

Then he could have lifted the building.

2

During the night a woman screamed. He thought he dreamed running footsteps and cursing and a woman crying. A man cursed God, called upon God to damn Himself. The woman's screams became cries, and the man's God-damning curses became sobs, choking sobs, each deeper than the one before. And there was the dull rhythmic thud of flesh on flesh.

Footsteps passed his door, then the crying woman, and the sobbing man. It was Blackie.

Her long fingers closed around his arm. She hid half awake down underneath him in his arms and moaned.

His eyes closed. Surely it was a dream.

3

He no longer thought of the ship or what she needed; he thought of the shore. When the Bosun declared the workday ended, he dropped whatever was in hand and headed for the shower. He was the first dressed, and the first into the messhall, and still chewing his supper and carrying a bag of fried egg sandwiches, he was the first down the gangway and into the bumboats. Money was his problem. The Captain allowed him only two thirds of his pay.

"But it's mine. I've already worked for it."

"It's the law. This is a foreign port. If you're paid in full, you might jump ship."

So he borrowed. But the longer they stayed in the river, the more everyone had drawn to the limit, and the less

there was to borrow. Someone told him to try the Steward,
but the fat Steward said, "What interest you pay? You got
collateral?"

"Sure I'll pay interest. Whatever you want. What do you
want?"

"I want collateral."

"My suitcase?"

"That cardboard box?"

So he tried the Satchel Man.

The Satchel Man leaning on the railing and looking
across the water at the lights of Joetown, didn't turn his
head. "You know what they call me. You know I don't
draw money in foreign ports."

"Just draw enough to lend me," he said. "Please."

"That bad?"

"Please."

He didn't want to say please. And each morning he left
her in the room with the baby telling himself he wouldn't
say please tonight. He walked through the morning's clear
light to the bumboat walkway telling himself he'd had
enough shore to last a lifetime. The brush of clothes against
his body pained him almost to sickness. This time he meant
it. No shore tonight. Every cell in his body was hungover.

He dragged through the day hiding from the Bosun. He
painted the bottoms of lifeboats, anything to find a moment
for his eyes to droop into sleep. Suspended in a sling above
the dark water he painted the *Ekonk*'s sides half awake and
half dreaming, his thoughts slipping into dreams and his
dreams into half-waking thoughts until he couldn't keep
track of time or even if he was dreaming or sleeping. When
the Bosun found him and said it was coffee time or lunch-
time, he plodded after him trying not to come awake. And

then in the afternoons after a hundred catnaps her body became more real in his hands than the paintbrush. Gazing seaward he could hardly breathe for the sudden ache in his groin. Behind closed eyes he porpoised in the night through her dark flesh.

He groaned.

"Please," he said.

The Satchel Man turned his swollen jaw. "I want to know exactly how much you need. I'll ration you."

Each night after mess, the brown bag of fried egg sandwiches in hand, he went to the Satchel Man.

"This is not my usual role," the Satchel Man said one night. "Mine's usually the underhand. I like this. I don't even think of myself ashore now. All I have to do is ponder your problem."

"Yessir," he said, waiting for the Satchel Man to quit talking and hold out the money.

"You ought to be patented and bottled," the Satchel Man said.

He quit listening. She didn't meet him at the bar anymore but waited for him in the room. He climbed the steps from the street, gave the woman in green the Satchel Man's money, and climbed the balcony stairs to her door.

First she ate the sandwiches. Then she nursed the baby. He sat on the floor beside her, his face lifted to the air coming off the river, and drank. She crooned and clucked and rocked the suckling child on her haunches. When the child finished she looked at him with luminous eyes. She crooned and clucked to him too, and he slept in an odor of milk and flesh and dreamed of a swelling sea. They awoke rocking in each other's arms. And slept again.

Sometimes in the morning's light he awoke to find the

bed empty and her curled on the floor. She smiled in sleep when he brought his pillow and curled, with bursting head, on the bare boards beside her.

"Girl, don't you know this floor is hard? Don't you like beds?" He stroked her long back and flanks — *Girl, I hope you know I'm crooning to you* — until she went back to sleep, and he awoke again and stumbled out the door.

Outside he sometimes met other *Ekonk* men. Once the Bosun, one foot down both feet on, descended the balcony stairs with two shoeshine boys.

"Morning, Kid," the Bosun said combing fingers through his thick, tousled hair.

On the narrow street the Bosun gave the boys money. With their shine boxes slinging their shoulders they counted the money with tiny hands.

He almost puked.

Waiting on the bumboat landing platform he couldn't look the Bosun in the eye. His head ached, and the touch of his breeches nauseated him. He kept seeing the tiny hands flicking the green bills. For sure he was not coming ashore tonight. For damned sure.

"My God, Boats," he said hoarsely.

The Bosun turned to him, but he still wouldn't look into the old face. "You think what you want to think," the Bosun said turning away. "Not that it is any of your business, but we play games together. That's all."

"Yes," he said. "Yes." Then he added in spite of himself. "The girl and I, we play games too."

"Go to hell," the Bosun said. "You're a stupid Kid. You think because you can now steer a straight course, paint, tie knots, and do a day's work you know things. All you know is steering and painting and tying and working."

Please?

And the Satchel Man rubbed his jaw and shook his head.

"Kid, there are things you don't know about Boats. You've heard him sing those songs in German. Do you know they're all children's songs? I think he really does play kid games with them. He's the way he is because that's the way he is. You beg for the girl because that's the way your needs are."

"Yessir."

And one morning he descended the split-log stairs to find Blackie lying half-naked in the street with one bare foot twisted and white on the curb. The silken hair shone on Blackie's chest, bare from the waist up. His belt had been ripped off, and his pants' pockets hung torn in the dirt and stones. Flies walked his face in and out of his gaping mouth.

He stood on the rock curb beside the foot watching the flies. He shook his head and went to the corner. Then he came back and pushed the foot into the street and tried to lift the dead weight of Blackie's shoulders. The head rolled, and the flies rose.

"C'mon, Blackie, get up."

He slapped the stubbled cheeks through the buzz of flies. Blackie only moaned. He snatched the hair from around Blackie's nipples.

"Hey!"

"C'mon now."

"Kid, hey, Kid."

Blackie clutched at his arm and pushed at the stones with his feet. Together they got him leaning erect and stumbling through the streets and down the narrow railless walkway to the bumboat landing. Beneath the swaying walkway the water rolled seaward.

He and the skinny oarsman got Blackie into the bumboat, where he curled on the bottom mumbling, "Won't forget this, Kid. Won't. No. Never."

Going up the gangway Blackie leaned back on him, half stumbling, half riding, and still mumbling, *Never, no.* Then Blackie saw Red waiting at the top of the gangway. "Goddamnit," Blackie cried lurching and pulling at the gangway chains, "leave me the hell alone." Blackie lurched onto the deck, telling Red in a loud voice, "He's a stupid punk."

He shook his head at Red and laughed.

Please?

The Satchel Man handed him the money, and he headed for the gangway with her dark flesh in his hands for another night. He hurried off the bumboat runway onto the shore. Across the street beneath the streetlight a shine boy knelt with his rags at the Bosun's feet.

Nausea churned his stomach. He hurried the other way, away from her and the Ice Chest.

"Shine, Meester?"

And from a shadowy alley, "Taxi? Taxi, Sailor?"

The bent driver sat high on the seat of a hansom cab behind a sleek bay. The cab's springs gave to his weight. "Anywhere, Driver. Let's ride." He threw the brown bag of fried egg sandwiches into the street.

They rode down one of Joetown's streets to the end of the streetlights, but they didn't stop there. The horse trotted down a dark road beyond the lights. The road wound among trees heavy against the night. At last lights appeared, and they turned into a palm-lined street with streetlights and large white houses that turned into a palm-lined street with streetlights and large white houses that turned into more palm-lined streets. They rode among grocery stores, drugstores, movie houses, and hotels. The lettering on a store window said in gold JOHNSTOWN HARD-WARE. On the canopy of a hotel was JOHNSTOWN HOTEL. Beneath the canopy the Cook talked with two men in white suits.

His heart leaped at the sight of the Cook's familiar face. "Stop," he cried. But by the time he'd paid the fare the Cook had disappeared into the hotel. With the black watch cap in hand he searched the cool lobby. He asked the clerk for the man who just came in: "The tall one in the Panama hat."

"Oh, you mean the Captain," the pointed-faced clerk said. "He's in four-o-seven."

"No, I mean the Cook not the Captain. The real tall man."

"With the angular face?"

"Yes, our cook."

The pointed-faced clerk talked into the ear of another clerk typing cards. The other clerk turned and studied him. "Do you know his name?"

"No. Just who he is."

"Well, I'm sorry."

He put his black watch cap on the back of his head. "It's O.K."

The clerks looked at his cap, then at each other. "If you want," one said, "you can call four-o-seven on the house phone."

He walked past the house phones and out the door. He no more wanted to see the Cook than he wanted to see the Bosun. What if he called 407, and the Cook answered? What would he say? Hi, Captain, are you the Cook? Or would it be better to say, Hi, Cook, are you the Captain?

Hell, he'd only wanted to see him because he was a familiar face in a strange place. Imagine him knowing somebody this far from Arkansas. He'd thought they might do
something together, see a movie maybe. Afterward they
could talk about it over a soda. But the Cook didn't want a
familiar face. He wanted strangers. Hell, he *needed* strangers. Most people needed friends to be who they were. The
Cook needed strangers to be what he wanted to be.

He crossed the paved street to a drugstore, but it wasn't
like a drugstore at all. No soda jerk worked a marble
counter. No long mirror hung the wall. Drugs lined shelves
behind glass cases filled with more drugs. Against a side
wall stood a Coca-Cola box with a block of ice melting on
the tops of upright bottles.

He sipped a Coke, leaned against a glass case, and talked
with the white-coated pharmacist who warned him that sailors weren't wanted outside of Joetown. "Over there it's anything goes. But over here we have rules." He took off his
watch cap and stuffed it inside his shirt.

But back on the street he felt naked without his cap and
cocked it on the back of his head as he studied the posters
outside a movie house. Inside the movie house he sat in the
dimness watching the screen beyond the dark heads. Lights
flicked but the screen was far away. He turned around.
Along the back wall heads were paired together, and above
the paired heads the movie flickered from a hole in the wall.
Overhead a bug flew the light. The screen was all flat and
far away with no one to share. He watched the pictures of
the young woman smiling and talking on the screen, and he
watched the other people watching the screen, and he
watched himself watching the screen and the other people.
He shook his head.

But his eyes would not focus.

"Sandwiches," he said to the ashen face beside him. "Fried egg sandwiches."

"What?"

He fled the movie house looking for a restaurant and the bent driver at the same time.

And the next morning he stumbled the streets with light breaking the water. His feet hit the narrow walkway and he waited on the platform bench with the water sliding beneath him.

He must have fallen asleep, waiting for the bumboat, for when he opened his eyes they were there. The Chief Mate and Blackie.

The Chief Mate was slapping Blackie, and Blackie was on his knees begging.

"Please," Blackie said, and the Mate hit him across the face with his open palm.

Blackie's head turned, and he began to cry.

"Please."

The Mate slapped him with his other hand.

"Please, Mate."

The Mate drove his closed fist into Blackie's upraised face. Blackie toppled backward to the edge of the platform, one hand hanging in the dark water. The Chief Mate began pissing over him and over the edge of the platform. The Mate streamed a link of water into the river, and in spite of himself the Kid looked. The Bosun was right. It was tattooed. It's head was red and yellow and it had wings tattooed on it. Water streamed into the river from a red-and-yellow butterfly.

The Mate peered sideways at him. "Bastard likes it," the Mate said. "I like to oblige."

"I noticed," the Kid said.

"Oh? You a smart Kid?"

The Mate rolled Blackie to a balance on the edge of the platform and held him there with his foot.

"Please," Blackie whispered into the wet planks. "Please."

"Want to help him, Kid? You like some of what he's getting?"

"Like you say, I'm a smart Kid."

"Then maybe you'd like it the other way. You want to pound him a while?"

"I see no pleasure in it."

"You're different, huh?"

"I'm sure not like you."

"You are exactly like me. Everybody likes to pound, and everybody likes to be pounded. They're the only things Blackie likes. Look, Kid, everybody's either wearing gold braid, or he isn't. That's a head-on fact and you're trying to slip around it."

"I've given orders," the Kid said. "And I've taken them, but they never filled me up with pleasure."

"Bull," the Mate said rolling Blackie beneath his foot. "Bull. That girl you're after. You never tried to pound her through the mattress? Not for one hot moment?"

"It's none of your business," the Kid said.

The Mate looked underneath his foot at Blackie. "Look, Kid, if I do it, you can too."

The next day he held out his hand to the Satchel Man at the afternoon coffee break, but the Satchel Man shook his swollen head and the Kid said again, "Why do you want me to beg?"

The Satchel Man shook his swollen head again and

pointed into the messroom where the Bosun sat. The Bosun put his jar of rum and tea on the table and crooked his finger at him.

"Kid," the Bosun said. "I want you to go ashore for me. I want you to take James to the dentist. You will take him there. You will wait for him. You will bring him back aboard."

"Yessir."

In the bumboat the Satchel Man leaned against him. On the walkway the Satchel Man walked a close step behind. On land the Satchel Man walked into his back when he stopped.

"My money," he said holding out his hand. "I'll have it now."

The Satchel Man shook his head and mumbled through his swollen jaw.

"What?"

The Satchel Man spoke slowly. "I said I told Boats you'd leave me for the girl, but he wouldn't believe me."

"The money," the Kid said. "Not a lecture."

The Satchel Man gave it to him in a wad already counted. While he stuffed it in his billfold, the Satchel Man headed across the street for a bar. The Kid grabbed his arm in the sunny middle of the street. "Hold now, you're going to the dentist," the Kid said.

In the Johnstown dental office he put the Satchel Man in a chair between a woman in blue and a woman in red flowers. He talked to the woman in white behind the glass. Then he gathered a stack of magazines from the table and dumped them into the Satchel Man's lap. "It'll be two hours," he said.

Back in Joetown she opened the door with surprise on

her face. The tension had drained from him at her first touch. She'd opened the door and lifted her long arms to his neck in surprise. He lay now across the bed beside her watching the baby.

Contented.

Outside this room they could all do what they pleased, be what they pleased. Be cooks or captains or victims or anything else. He was where he wanted to be. With a start he realized it was true. Given his choice of being any place on earth or any person on earth, he would choose in this room and him with her. She dangled a cloth beyond the baby's waving hands, and he closed his eyes. The bare length of her moved against his side. God he was sleepy. If only there was some way to come ashore every afternoon. To love her and rest.

Tomorrow.

Tomorrow was far away, but he would do it tomorrow. He'd find the geezer that spoke her language, find out about her. What she needed. If she had any people, and how to get her back to them. Ireland. Hell, if the shamrock weighed more it could get her there, but if it weighed a ton it wouldn't find her dead father's spirit. He'd cursed her with his shamrock charm. Her life would be drained out in this place. Not all the men would treat her as he did. Now there was a thought. What was so different about him? Wasn't he treating her as they would? The same as Gus or Gene or Blackie, except Blackie would always have to beat her or have her beat him. Gus too. And him too. One night he *had* tried to drive her through the mattress. He beat her body, and she began to beat back until they both lay exhausted in sweat. Afterward she had never been more gentle and kind, and he had trembled at her every touch.

Because it was with him it was all right, but he didn't
take care of her. The woman in green did that. Aboard
ship they were men without women. Here they were
women without men. That was why he had to do something tomorrow. Tomorrow he would find the geezer. Get
it all straightened out.

She moved dimly beside him, and he tried to open his
eyes, but it was too much trouble. The weight of her left
the bed. When her weight returned, he opened his eyes
onto the baby waving in his box. He watched the waving
hands and wondered what was strange. Then he wondered
what he was wondering about. He studied the shadows on
the floor, then fell to wondering about the lights of the ships
on the river. He turned on his back. The overhead light
haloed her black hair.

His rush in dressing frightened her. He made a soothing
gesture and ran out the door.

The dentist's office was locked. The cab driver took him
to the nearest bars, but these bars were in hotels and restau-
rants. The Satchel Man wouldn't be in these places, and
even if he was it was too dark to see him.

Back in the well-lighted bars of Joetown he searched the
dark faces, but he couldn't find him. After a while he realized each of the bars had an upstairs like the Ice Chest.

"Shine, Meester?"

He shook his head through corner lights back to the Ice
Chest. The *Ekonk* crew had arrived. The Bosun signaled to
him, but he shook his head and mounted the stairs to the
balcony. When she opened the door he touched her shoulder and threw himself across the bed. He lay there seeing
the Satchel Man lying drunk anywhere from Johnstown to
Joetown, being in jail, rolled, beaten, and finally being left

behind when the *Ekonk* sailed. And he had done it. If he
had waited — if he'd waited, he'd be here fresh from the
ship and they'd be in each other's arms right now. All he'd
done was make something happen a few hours before it
would happen anyway. And at what cost?

She touched his cheek. He caught her hand and tumbled
her across him onto the bed. Her eyes widened at his de-
manding fierceness. He forced her clothes and legs like a
rapist, and she caught his face in her palms trying to make
him look into her eyes, but he jerked his head away. Her
hands dropped. Her head turned sideways on the bed, and
she stilled beneath him. When he finished, she pushed him
aside, went into the bathroom, and closed the door.

Listening to the water splashing the rose-covered tub, he
closed his eyes and disappeared in a wave of sleep. But a
baby's cry troubled his dreams. The baby's cries quickened
until there was the sharp slap of flesh on flesh. The baby
cried even louder.

The cries rose, many cries. The cries of men. Men shouting and cursing, feet running the street, and someone shouting *Ekonk! Ekonk!*

He raised his head from the bed. Beyond the empty crib
the street was full of men. The mass of men roiled like
water around the Satchel Man, who reeled in the middle of
the street head down and barely able to stand. They were
stripping him, tearing away his clothes, yanking and beating
his body.

He leaped from the bed. She stood in the bathroom door
framed in light holding the baby to her dark cheek.
"They've got him," he cried to her and ran down the balcony pulling on his clothes as he went.

He took the stairs in long leaps. The last leap jumped

him into the middle of the *Ekonk* crew. Led by Gene and
Gus the crew was running across the dance floor. Gus and
Gene hit the outside stairway together, and they all followed. He ran down the split-log steps beside Slim the
Oiler. Slim's mouth was open, and everybody's mouth was
open, and he heard himself yelping, giving tongue the way
his father urged hunting dogs. In full cry they poured into
the mass of dark bodies. Gus clubbed his arms to open the
way. He followed surrounded by *Ekonk* crewmen and they
drove to the center of the street. The Satchel Man's shirt
was torn away, and he was crying. The Kid clamped an arm
over the Satchel Man's shoulders, and the Satchel Man
clutched his other arm to his chest. Then Gus and Gene
turned them around, and it became a running street fight.
Gus and Gene, clubbing their fists, drove them against the
dark bodies, but instead of giving, the mass of bodies moved
with them down the street. They moved within a moving
mass. Everybody was swinging and kicking at the roil of
bodies around them. Beneath a streetlight the fight spread
into the cross of streets. And now the dark bodies were running ahead to block the bumboat walkway. Again he became aware of the roar of voices. He ran with the Satchel
Man down an open throat. Then in a trick of ear the one
throat became many: shouting, cursing.

"Look out, Red."

He couldn't find Red.

"Oh NO!"

"FUCK."

Gene ran alongside a dark face rhythmically punching it
every other step until the face dropped away. Gus ran
straight into a small tattered man and over him. The small
dark face tilted slowly backward as though studying the
stars and was gone.

Then he was shoved from behind, and the Satchel Man slipped away. He tripped on a curb and stumbled off-balance into a man with clenched white teeth. Light flickered from the teeth, and the same light flickered from the blade of the knife in the man's raised hand. He reached for the knife with both hands. His fingers twisted among smaller fingers onto the warm bone handle, and, still stumbling, his lowered head butted into the clenched teeth. With a shiver the man's body relaxed. He twisted, pulled the knife free from the smaller fingers, found his balance, and raced to catch the others.

His feet barely touched the street. Someone ran at him with widespread arms. In two quick bounds he was around the man, who ran on down the street with his arms still out. Then out of the corner of his eye came a rock from beyond the streetlight, arching down toward his head and spinning from right to left. He slowed slightly and the rock turned past the end of his nose. Its brown edges were dull and chipped.

Lights gleamed on the river, and the mass of bodies thickened. Gene and Gus were on either side of the bumboat walkway clubbing the dark faces as the *Ekonk* crew slipped between them and crossed the water to the safety of the platform. Peewee half carried the Satchel Man across, and Red helped Blackie, whose head was bloody.

Gene was yelling at him, "Run, Kid, Run!"

Arms wrapped him from behind, and he struck backward into the stomach with his fist. To his surprise the arms slid away. But several of them separated him from the walkway twenty yards ahead. There was no other way. He ran straight at them and sprang. The middle one caught him in midair and folded him in his arms.

"KID." The cry was sharp as an order.

The arms tightened. His nose touched the dark nose before him. Brown eyes smiled into his, and their cheeks
pressed together as his back bent and his toes touched the
stone street. Someone hit him in the back of the head and
his cheek turned. The breath from between the grinning
uneven teeth blew sweetish and lemony on his cheek. His
own breath exploded from his tightening rib cage, and he
weakly beat his fists against the muscled back. Again and
again he pounded the back with his fists. The lips over the
uneven teeth thickened into a grimace. With a slow groan
the arms loosened from his chest. He spun free and ran between Gus and Gene. The walkway swayed to his feet.

They yelled for the bumboats out among the ships, and as
the boats came back they took turns defending the narrow
walkway. He ran back onto the walkway crying *Let me,
Let me,* but Gene, laughing, dragged him back. He threw
off Gene's arms, bounced from foot to foot, watched the
dripping oars flash with light. He wanted to run out and
push the boats in.

Oars were slow.

He lifted his foot to step onto the water when the Bosun
took his shoulder.

"Calm down, Kid. You are all right now."

"Boats," he cried. "Godamighty. Oh godamighty."

The first boat bumped the platform. They shoved at each
other to be the first aboard. Then two more boats banged
the platform, and they were all aboard with Gene making
the last boat in a running leap.

Back aboard the *Ekonk* they milled around the gangway
talking, boasting.

"Did you see me . . ."

"Two of them . . ."

The Kid hopped from foot to foot. It had not been enough; he was not satisfied. He talked excitedly to anyone and no one. He threw arms around the Bosun, but Gus grabbed him. Gus twisted his arms from the Bosun's neck and bent him to his knees. The crew, all silent now and watching, stepped back, and then Gus released him, and Gus stepped back.

He was on his knees in the middle of a circle.

"Kid," Gus said. "You can throw the knife over the side now."

"What?" he said. "What?"

"In your hand," the Bosun said.

He looked down at his raising hands. The long red blade dripped from the bottom of one fist. His right hand was locked to the bone handle. He watched the man's smile turn into a grimace as he plunged the knife again and again into his muscled back.

"No," he groaned. "No."

And he felt the other pair of arms slide away when he plunged the knife backward into the stomach.

"No."

They helped him to his feet, and then they had to help him open his fist. He held the knife out over the side, but the hand wouldn't open. One by one Gus pried loose his fingers until the knife turned down to the dark water.

Then he ran for his curtained bunk.

And as he lay there, he was sure he remembered feeling the knife in his hand and hadn't he seen it flash as he drove it into the man's back? Or had he? Anyway, he'd done it. Whether he'd known or not, his hand had known. His hand had acted. At that moment he had been his hand, acting willfully and out of fear.

The Mate was right; he had it all in him too.
And he had loved it.

After he ran, they discovered the sailing orders posted on
the board at the head of the gangway. He was still behind
his makeshift curtain when, in the morning's first light, the
Ekonk wound her anchor from the river bottom. They
hosed the river mud from the chain and laid it in its locker.

And while the *Ekonk* pushed upriver, he lay in his bunk
staring open-eyed at the metal plate beside him.

They tried without success to get him out of his bunk and
working.

"At least you're not hungover," Red said. "A big fight
gets the crew sober. Why don't you answer me?"

He stared at the metal plate until the engine stopped and,
after much yelling and footsteps, started again. After a
while the engine stopped again.

The Bosun pulled back his curtain. "Come on, Kid. We
need your help." The Bosun lifted his legs over the side of
the bunk, and he sat up. "We are aground in the river," the
Bosun said handing him his cutoff khakis. As he pulled
them over his legs the Bosun spoke in a quiet voice, "When
the tide goes out, we go aground in the shallow spots. We
have to pull her free and go on. Coming back out loaded
with ore we will stay aground when the tide is out. Come
on now. Every hand is needed."

The Bosun took down from the shelf the leather gloves already in the shape of his hands. He pulled them on, smell-
ing the dark sweat and kneading the bull-hide stiffness into
his flesh.

On deck he had to look high to see the sky. Green jungle
leaned solidly over the river. Ahead a great boled tree had

leaned too far, and the dark water pushed through its bending limbs. He climbed down a Jacob's ladder into a lifeboat,
and they towed the ship's hawsers into the green under-
growth, bent them around the trees, and winched the
Ekonk off the land. They hauled her free, started the propeller, and rode her to the next shallow place. There they
climbed back into the boats, tied her to the jungle trees, and
hauled her free again. When the tide came in, they rode
and rested. And when in the night the tide went out, they
climbed back into the boats. They hauled her ablaze with
lights deeper into the night. She sailed into the heart of the
jungle with running lights lit and lookouts posted.

All night the Captain walked the bridge, hatless, coatless.
And all night the Chief Mate stayed on the focslehead.
The Mate worked the winches himself, worked wherever
the pull was hardest. He and the Bosun tested the deck
with their feet and told them where to tie the hawsers. And
when they were tied, the winches billowed steam, and the
Mate worked and cursed.

As the lighted ship passed, the jungle quietened. They
heard only the sounds of the ship, except once. He and
Gene, wrestling a thick wet hawser into place around a tree,
found it full of monkeys, newly awakened and excited.

And once as he and the Satchel Man rested side by side
on a hatch, the Satchel Man said. "Kid, did the knife scare
you?"

"Yes."

"Still?"

"Yes."

"Then you don't have to be too scared."

"Yes I do. I got it in me too. The Mate's right. It's not
something out yonder. It's inside."

After a while the Satchel Man said, "We're all capable." And still later he said, "Kid?"

"Yes?"

"I wanted you to leave me in the dental office. Don't you know that? I was making the live things in my jaw, and you, do my deciding. Then I could blame you, and the crew would feel sorry for me."

"Did the dentist help?"

"I left right after you did, and my head hurts."

And coming back out of the jungle with the *Ekonk*'s belly full of red earth, they ran aground and they stayed aground until the tide pushed back into the jungle and freed them.

Waiting for the tide to float them free they sat in the deckhands' focsle telling stories, drinking coffee, tying Tomfool knots that had no purpose other than the tying. Blackie came in holding aloft two large dark bottles.

"Rum," Blackie cried.

Coffee cups were emptied, toothbrush glasses dumped. Blackie circled the room pouring. "Saw me this dugout canoe under the fantail. Lowered an old pair of dungarees in a bucket. Hauled up rum. How about that?"

"You performed a miracle," Gene said.

Blackie poured the last of the rum into his own glass and lifted it. "A short trip and a long life."

"Aye."

They tossed down the rum. All except Blackie, who studied his glass. When they lowered their glasses, Blackie lifted from his glass a leggy, two-inch cockroach pickled in rum.

"And to the cockroaches in the rum," Blackie said and drank.

They cursed Blackie while laughing. They hunted through their belongings for old clothes. Soon several canoes floated beneath the fantail, and on deck were a dozen stalks of bananas, a stack of coconuts, three more bottles of rum, and in cages, a monkey and two gaudy parrots.

The Kid sipped rum and tea from a jar and watched the trading. It would be an easy matter to lower himself over the side and buy a whole canoe. How far? Five hours paddling downstream. Three fried egg sandwiches from the bar, and —

Or was he wanted for murder?

Maybe the whole crew.

Then the tide came in and floated them free.

The Kid paced the focslehead on watch as the *Ekonk,* with running lights lit, slid under the night. Toward the end of his watch they rounded a bend, and there were the lights of Joetown. The shore lights ran like paths to the ship's side and the lights of the Ice Chest stood above the others. He could see the windows, and wondered if she was standing in one. He'd meant to do something. But what? He went to the railing, wondering how he could get ashore. Perhaps with a big life jacket on he could . . The bell from the bridge rang seven times. Turning, he checked the *Ekonk's* running lights and answered with the watch bell's clapper.

Dong-dong
Dong-dong
Dong-dong
Dong

Cupping his hands to his mouth, he sang, "Lights are bright, sir."

Thank you.

Holding the clapper he watched Joetown slide by, knowing he couldn't swim it. How many times was this to hap-

pen in his life? A lover found, a friend made, a battle
fought? For the rest of his life she would live in the room,
blue eyes unfaded, long body always supple; and her baby
would sleep always in the tiny box. His stomach wrenched.
Only he would change. Other people would be frozen into
his life while he went on ringing bells, checking running
lights, doing whatever it took to keep pushing ahead.

He watched the lights of Joetown recede until his relief
climbed the focslehead at eight bells. By then Joetown was
a bright reflection on the horizon clouds. He left the focslehead not wanting to go inside yet, not wanting to see the
lights disappear. He stopped at the after well deck railing
and leaned there with the beginning of sea swells pushing
his feet.

The Mate stepped from a passageway with the parrot
cage in one hand and the monkey cage in the other. With
two small thuds the Mate balanced the cages on the railing
beside him. Gnarled parrot feet climbed the bars upside-
down, and the monkey stirred sleepily in one corner.

With the heels of his hands the Mate pushed both the
cages over the railing into the water.

The boxes somersaulted the air, and the parrots screamed.
But he heard her baby screaming. He saw her baby spill
from its box and her grabbing frantically through the air for
the baby but she couldn't reach him. The golden shamrock
fell from her neck, the baby disappeared, and behind her
falling hair her eyes, dulled and faded in a face wrinkled
with age, turned from his.

Again the two parrots screamed, and the cages bobbed aft
through the glow of lights. The monkey's furry arm reached
out between the bars for the ship as the last of her hair sank
beneath the water.

It's what he had done.

"Goddamn you, MATE!"

The Mate was halfway down the deck.

"Try throwing me over the side!"

The Mate considered for a moment. "What's the matter, Kid? It was just a couple of parrots and a monkey."

"Fight ME," the Kid cried.

"Stupid Kid," the Mate said laughing over his shoulder. "I'm not running a menagerie. You guys would have pets all over our decks and you'd let the seas clear them." The Mate went on across the deck and disappeared.

After a while he heard the sound of his breathing and of the ship throbbing.

From the railing he looked around the deck at the neatly battened hatches, the lashed booms, everything shipshape and sea-ready. And he tried to remember the long length of her against his body, the taste of her milky breasts, the curl of arms around his neck. But her memory was mixed with the odor of sweetish lemony breath blowing between the uneven teeth as the man's back muscles jerked under the slip of the knife.

He left the deck.

Back in his focsle he climbed quietly into his bunk as the Satchel Man moaned in sleep. He pressed his wind-warmed cheek to the *Ekonk*'s metal plate and tried not to listen to the moans or to think. Pressing the cool metal, he listened to the ship gurgling the sea, and he fell asleep thinking that hitting the Mate wouldn't have changed his hurt, nor would have being hit. It would only have made him forget for a moment that his life was something he carried in his head like a cargo. Only *it* did not change.

During the night, for the first time in his life, he turned and groaned in his sleep.

Homeward

1

HOMEWARD BOUND the *Ekonk* sailed through low heavy seas for a while and, for a while, through a calm. It was during the calm that the *Ekonk*'s great engine was stopped and the crew gathered bareheaded at the railing to bury the Satchel Man, who died one night in his bunk.

The Kid awoke one day during the heavy seas with his feet pressed to the foot railing and pillows bracing his shoulders. He lay wedged in his pitching bunk wondering if it was day or night. Then he found he'd fallen asleep in his cutoff khakis. He took his work gloves from the foot of the bunk and went into the messroom.

"I was about to give you a call," Gene said over his coffee cup.

"It's another day," the Kid said.

Peewee came in grumbling about the Steward wanting him to carry hot food across flooded decks and began slamming drawers in preparing the messroom for supper. Blackie stuck his head in the door. "Hey, Kid. Bosun told me to lash down a barrel. One of the blackgang left it portside amidships. My watch is up. How about you catching it. He's up forward painting inside."

"Yeah, sure."

He finished a coffee and went out on deck with Gene. They dogged the door shut behind them and hopped on a hatch to avoid the sloshing water. The seas quartered in from the bow low and heavy. But because of the *Ekonk's* heavy load, the waves sloshed her lower decks. He and Gene crossed the hatch and, between waves, crossed to the next hatch, then ran for the midships ladder and climbed clear.

"See you," Gene said and climbed on toward the bridge. He crossed through the midship housing swaying from wall to wall. He undogged a portside door, stepped out on deck, and dogged the door behind him.

The *Ekonk* rolled to port. He grabbed the handles of a two-foot-thick ventilator as the fifty-gallon steel drum skidded from a corner behind a ladder. The barrel skidded past him down to the chain railing. A hump of blue-green water rolled a foot beneath the deck. He held the ventilator handles and waited for the barrel to come back. When it did, he tossed a hand line over it and took a turn round the ventilator.

As he dodged, the barrel rolled around on its ten-foot leash. But he couldn't get the leash shortened. He tried to get the drum into the corner again, get it wedged there, then lash it to the ladder leading up to the boat deck. The barrel tilted, and the line slipped.

He went after the barrel with the limp line.

He slid down the wet deck to the railing, but the barrel rolled out of reach. With one hand on the railing he tossed the line like a lasso.

His feet were wet. He glanced over the row after row of long heavy waves coming in, then he leaned into the tilt of deck for the ventilator. He pushed his way up the tilt and pulled himself behind the ventilator just in time for the deck to tilt the other way and the barrel to skid past into the corner.

"KID!"

The Mate was hollering through cupped hands.

"KID!"

On the deck above, the Mate's silk kimono blew stiffly away from his naked body. The Mate windmilled both arms at him.

Suddenly he was stumbling up the ladder with his heart beating his throat.

"Stupid Kid," the Mate shouted helping him to his feet. "What you —"

"Boats told me to."

The *Ekonk* pitched and lay down to port.

They grabbed for each other, locked their arms together, and spread their feet. On the lower deck blue-green water humped beneath the chain railing then over the middle strand. The solid water crossed the deck, hit the corner, and shot straight up. The water stood bright and crackling before their faces. They held each other and saw in the water, close enough to touch, the rusting barrel with its sides crushed over a rung of the ladder. Then the barrel dropped and washed over the side with the hissing water.

The ladder tilted awry with its bottom rungs missing.

He looked down at the empty deck.

"Let go," the Mate said pushing at his arm.

Looking upon the wet emptiness he kept hearing the crackling.

"Let go damnit."

"Oh. Excuse me." He braced himself against a lifeboat davit. "Blackie told me Boats said . . ."

"To hell with the Bosun. He's an old man. You think before you listen to him. Because he hasn't got what it takes anymore, he doesn't believe it takes anything."

"How's that?"

"You just saw it. Do you need a diagram? Do you see him out on deck dodging waves? No, he's inside. You're still the same stupid Kid he sent aloft to paint. Do you know how long it's been since he was aloft? He doesn't remember what's up there. He's an old man remembering a dream."

"I'll never forget being aloft that day. Or what he gave me that day."

The Mate snorted and scratched the bird clawing his left elbow. "And you — you'll get old and turn it all into a dream too. Christ, you've already started. Look around you," the Mate cried sweeping his arm at the sea. "Don't you know what's waiting? Didn't you hear the damn water standing there snarling at us. Old men," the Mate said turning away in disgust. "Deaf old men and stupid Kids."

He went aft to the messroom and drank coffee. After a while the Bosun came to the messroom across the flooded decks. Each day afterward he waited for the Bosun to come to him, and while the Bosun told him what needed to be done, he heard also the water's crackling voice. As the wind died the water lay calm and inert around the ship but behind the water's calm surface he knew the voice was still there, and never again would he let someone make him forget it.

The calmer the sea became, the more he remembered.

The wind shifted around to the stern and matched the *Ekonk's* wallowing speed. The heat and soot and odors of the boiler fires poured from the smokestack and hung the air. They sailed enclosed inside their own waste and the longer they stayed in it, the thicker it hung. They tied handkerchiefs around their faces and coughed and cursed. The Captain staggered from his cabin in his pajamas, looked at the pall around them, and retreated behind his door.

When at last the trailing wind stilled, they sailed from beneath the pall into a murky sea and sky of a single inseparable blue. The sea lay about them with only slight swells moving beneath its unbroken surface. Then even the swells flattened, and the whole sea lay flat and the only ripple in the murky expanse of sea and sky was the *Ekonk's* wake.

They sat on the fantail and checked each other's steering by the long wake disappearing up the horizonless sky.

Blackie's wake trailed the stern like a snake.

"He's not concentrating," Red said laughing. "Maybe he's in no hurry to get home."

"Who would be to get where he's going," Slim the Oiler said. "He told me his old man is a Philadelphia cop. That his old man is the one sent him up. Manslaughter. Told me it was his brother. When he was fifteen."

"Jesus."

"Told me about it on watch the other night."

"So what?" Red said. "He still can't steer worth shit."

Wanting to show them he was good, the Kid concentrated hard on his steering. He buried his head in the binnacle and saw only the needle. He tried hard and after each watch he hurried aft to check his wake. One morning he hurried through the balmy dark under a yellow moon full in the murky sky. He rushed to the fantail railing right above the thumping propeller.

As usual he was disappointed. His wake was never as straight as he thought it would be. He looked into the water churning and flashing from the propeller. He was tired. He leaned both elbows on the railing and relaxed, glad his watch was about over. His legs ached from standing at the wheel for the past two hours.

With a foot on the lower railing he felt the warm night. Going home.

To the mountains. It was about over now. He must remember to take the seashells from the cardboard suitcase and drop them over the side. He'd leave them here where they came from, and he'd go back.

Something touched his face.

At first he thought it imagination.

It touched his face again, finer than any mist.

He concentrated and found it real. Something moved mistlike over his cheeks and eyes and lips and tickled inside his ears.

He lifted his face.

Its touch grew stronger, covered his bared shoulders, moved down his arms and over his stomach, caressing him. His eyes closed. It was delicious. The most wonderful thing in the world would be to have it all over his body, down his spine, between his toes, in his mouth. He wanted more.

He leaned over the railing.

Behind closed lids he saw himself fall slowly through the balmy air into the great mattress of water, have the warm water enfold him, enclose every pore, flow over and around every hair as though each hair itself was held in caress. His skin tingled. His stomach turned weak, and his mouth turned sweet as sugar.

White-knuckled hands clutched the railing.

"It's spray!" he shouted.

"Spray," he cried realizing with terror that he had nearly jumped. He looked down into the *Ekonk*'s wake. "Spray from the prop."

He backed from the railing and went on stumbling feet into the messroom. But the *Ekonk* was fully loaded. How could buried propellers throw airborne spray? His hands trembled around the coffee cup. What had Red told him, one hand for the ship and one for yourself. *So you won't jump.* Lifting his cup he knew he would wonder for the rest of his life what had really happened. Where had sea mist come from on a windless night?

2

That night as the Kid turned in his bunk and dreamed of jumping overboard, the Satchel Man lay dying in his bunk.

The lump in the Satchel Man's jaw had swollen to the size of a grapefruit. It throbbed now between his ears, and in the semidarkness of the focsle the engine pounded the pillow against his skull. He heard in the pillow all the ship's motors and pipes and valves. The ship throbbed his head, and the Satchel Man began steering. He set his feet to the deck and set his hands to the spokes, and he steered. Forty-foot waves rode out of nowhere to stand before his bow. They stood there with curling, hissing tops waiting to break. He steered into them, and the waves broke over him. They hit the ship and pounded her against his head. His whole body shuddered.

Except for his eyes, he lay paralyzed.

He remembered opening his eyes after midnight and finding he couldn't move. Then he remembered collapsing in the wheel house on watch yesterday. He'd felt the spokes slipping from his hands as he sank to his knees on the grating. They'd helped him to his bunk. The afternoon's rest made him feel better. He'd swallowed a little soup for supper, then slept until after midnight. After midnight he awoke, able to move only his eyes.

He looked across the light of the binnacle and through the glass of the wheel house at the next wave. He waited for the wave to break and pound his head. But it didn't. Across the binnacle light the Kid's curtain stirred. He fastened his eyes to the curtain. The Kid's bare legs emerged one at a time.

He moaned at the legs.

The Kid's head came out but didn't turn his way. The Kid rubbed his eyes with the heels of his hands and slid bare feet to the deck.

He moaned again.

The Kid slid his feet into wooden clogs and dragged a pair of khakis from behind the curtain.

The lump throbbed and shook him to his toes. He set his eyes on the Kid's face and concentrated. Why didn't the Kid hear him? The Kid was going on watch, that meant it was three-twenty. For three hours and twenty minutes he'd steered through the waves and tried to get someone's attention with his eyes and moans but no one heard him. Maybe he only thought he was moaning. Maybe he wasn't making a sound. He thought about that. The thought turned and turned in his head until it became mixed up with the pounding of the waves and the ship and his head, and he forgot what he was thinking about.

He took a deep breath, but no air filled his lungs.

Instead of air swelling his chest, a wave rose before the bow of the ship and stood there. He set his feet to the deck and his hands to the spokes.

The narrow bow disappeared into the base of the wave, and the wave broke. As he spun the spokes to catch her, the wave shuddered against the steel sides. His body shuddered with it. The wave rode its length beneath his feet, and he thought he would never make it through.

Then the rudder caught, and he and the ship rode free.

The next wave rose before him, and he studied it with fear. He concentrated hard, and in its depths he saw the Kid pushing a foot through the khakis.

He moaned.

He felt no air leave his lungs and vibrate his throat. He couldn't feel his throat. His body down there was only a shuddering extension to the throbbing in his head. From his pillow he studied his chest.

His eyes raised. He was no longer breathing.

KID. *Kid, look this way. Turn your head to me. Hear ME.*

Me. Me. But he was no longer me. Something was missing. Where was *she?* Down in his crotch the warmth from his bladder spread his thighs.

He forced himself to breathe, and as air hit his lungs, a green wave stood before him. He set his feet to the deck and his hands to the spokes. The narrow bow danced and slid inside the wave. He shuddered as the Kid's face leaned over the binnacle and smiled at him and said something he couldn't understand.

KID.

The Kid leaned over the binnacle and patted his hand on

the spoke. Warmth flooded his arm. The Kid's blue eyes smiled at him as he stared into their blue depths. Down in their reflecting depths he saw two mad eyes staring fiercely back, and he saw his fierceness soften as a little girl with blue eyes touched cold hands to his cheeks.

I see me in your eyes, she said.

He moaned.

He could have stood it if she had died. He could have accepted that. But walking around knowing that while he walked and breathed she too walked and breathed. No! His heart couldn't bear it. One night in his pain he dreamed that he found the town she lived in with her mother and that he killed her to bear it. The next day he quit job, and life, and fled. When he came to the end of the land he boarded a ship and went farther.

I see me in your eyes, Daddy.

He smiled into her blue eyes, and the blue eyes smiled back.

"Good," the Kid said. "I'm real glad you're better. Boats told me to take your watch for you later. Okay?"

He blinked.

Go away, Kid. You're in the way.

The Kid's blue eyes receded over the binnacle, and as the Kid's eyes receded, so did hers.

KID.

The Kid walked through the glass of the wheel house and disappeared into the waves.

He tried one more time to call up her eyes.

Her face?

Her hands?

Her voice?

Anything.

A wave stood before him.

Looking at the wave he thought of all the years he'd trained his mind to see waves instead of her. Now when he wanted her, he got waves.

He set his feet and hands.

Down below the Fireman tended his fires; the Oiler oiled the engine; and the Engineer regulated their speed. On the wing of the bridge a pair of eyes was on lookout. The Mate in the chart room watched their position. He was underway.

He looked down the binnacle's light and studied the compass. The needle swung. His breath caught, and he looked up into the next wave.

They came single file. They rose before the bow with curled crests frothing and hissing. He steered the bow inside them, and they broke, falling fiery and iridescent upon him. He shuddered through them, one after the other. There was no end to them. Each one was different. Each with a different problem.

The waves were in no hurry. They took their time. They rose before his bow. They stood there waiting for him to steer inside them. And *he* waited. He waited for his breath to catch and set the pounding throb of pain starting in his head. When the pain came, he nosed inside the wave, and the wave broke over him. He and the ship and the wave shuddered together until finally he came through to the other side to bob idly on blue water. When he tried to breathe again, another wave stood before him.

Where was he going?

He could think of no name for the ship. He could not remember any other crewmen. Was he the only man aboard?

Where WAS he going?

He studied the horizon for answer.

And then he saw it.

Four waves away stood the largest wave he had ever seen. It rose above the others like a mountain above hills. Watching it fearfully, he hardly noticed shuddering through the first of the three waves separating them.

Then he lost his fear of the great wave. He wanted only to get to it, and he plunged into the second wave without waiting. He and the ship and the wave shuddered together until he was almost exhausted. Then he bobbed free and started to rest. But the third wave came now to him. It broke over him before he was ready, and the bow swung wildly. He would never catch her. The third wave was one long throb of pain that had no end.

Then the rudder caught, and again he bobbed free.

The great wave stood now before his bow.

It stood astride the whole world. He studied it wondering how any ship could get through. He took a deep breath, and when he did the wave grew higher. Its crest curled above him, white and sparkling with phosphorus.

His narrow bow bobbed uncertainly. It nuzzled the wave's base, hesitated. He eased the spokes and held her steady to the wave. The bow slid inside.

He looked up the wave's side, up the white-curled crest, up to the blue sky above, and waited for the pain to come and the crest to break.

But the wave never broke.

3

When Gene and the Kid came aft after their watch, they found everyone standing around the after deck instead of inside eating breakfast. The Fat Fireman's either hand was filled with a pancake rolled around a wad of bacon. He chewed from one hand then the other.

"What the hell got you away from the table?" Gene asked.

"Hush," the Bosun said. "It is James. I just found him dead."

"Died in his sleep," the Fat Fireman said. "Peacefully. Didn't make a sound."

"Probably didn't even wake up," Red said.

"Hush," the Bosun said. "I know he was alive half an hour ago. I saw his hands moving."

"And I talked with him," the Kid said. "When I went on watch. I talked with him, touched him. He even smiled at me."

"Then you were the last one he talked to," the Bosun said. "I must go tell the Mate. Gene, you and Gus carry him to my locker amidships."

The Bosun shuffled his six-inch steps up the deck. Gus and Gene went into the focsle. Everyone else crowded in behind them.

The Satchel Man had on a pair of soiled skivvies.

"You take the feet," Gus said.

Gene picked up the feet, Gus the hands. His arms and legs rose, but the rest of the Satchel Man stayed in the bunk. They both climbed into the bunk with him. They pushed and pulled and all three of them came out of the bunk together. Gene had his bare legs under his arms, and Gus had him by the armpits. His head hung back so far he seemed to be studying the deck between Gus's legs.

"His hands are dragging," Gus said. "Pick up his hands."

"Hell," Gene said, "he'll never know the difference."

"I said don't let 'em drag."

"Pick up his hands," Gene said.

The Kid picked up his hands and folded them over the rib cage. The hands slid back to the deck.

"Dragging," Red said.

The Kid picked them up and stuffed them into the dirty skivvies as the Satchel Man folded like an accordion to the deck. Gene and Gus hitched at him and the hands fell out of the skivvies.

"Dragging," Red said.

"Damnit, Kid, don't let his hands drag the dirty deck," Gus said.

"Then hold him higher," the Kid said. They hitched him higher while the Kid picked up his hands and placed them one over the other on the hollowed stomach and held them. Under the pressure of his hand the Satchel Man sagged at the middle.

"Sagging," Red said.

"Shit," Gene said.

"Trying to help," Red said.

"Well don't," Gene said.

At the door they couldn't all get through at the same time.

"Christ, he weighs a ton," Gus said.

"No," Gene said, "it's just he ain't packaged for carrying." Gene hitched and grunted. "God. Imagine if the Fat Fireman died."

"Fuck you," the Fat Fireman said.

The Kid let go the hands and stepped aside to let them through the doorway. Gene stepped over the foot-high coaming.

"Hey," a voice outside cried, "you're letting his hands drag."

"Shit," Gene said.

Gus exploded. "Goddamnit, Kid, I told you."

"That's no way to carry him," Red said. "Somebody go get a hatch board."

They laid him on deck and waited for the hatch board. When the hatch board came, they rolled him on it. Gus lifted one end and Gene the other, and he promptly rolled off on deck with a thud.

"Ornery to the end," Gene said.

"Ornery, hell, you're just clumsy. Now let's do it right." Gus said.

The Kid held him on the board as they lifted it again. A bare arm slid off, and the Kid got it back; then the other arm slid, and finally both legs dangled.

"Dragging."

Gus began shaking his head, and his voice was empty of anger. "We got nearly a whole crew here. Can't we at least carry, not drag, the old man to his grave?"

"Somebody get on the other side," the Kid said.

Red got on the other side, but at the ladder both he and the Kid had to step aside. Gene went up first. The Satchel Man slid back down the board into Gus's arms.

"Hold, Gene."

Gene backed down the ladder.

"I'll have to carry him," Gus said.

They got the board out of Gus's hands and left the Satchel Man heaped in his arms. Gus hitched at him and the Satchel Man's legs slid astride one of Gus's arms and his arms around Gus's neck.

"Look out, Gus, he's attacking you."

"Don't stand there looking," Gus cried. "Help me."

"Put him down," the Kid said.

They helped Gus lay him on the board. "Now," the Kid

said, "let's stand him up so Gus can get him over his shoulders."

"You can't stand up a dead man," the Fat Fireman said.

"Do what the Kid says. He is the only one thinking," Gus said.

The Kid and Gene and Red tried to get him standing so Gus could get him on his back. They finally got him sagging a little more than on his knees.

Red grunted. "I keep wanting to ask him to help a little."

"Me too," the Kid said, and he and Red and Gene all three began giggling.

"Shut up and lift," Gus said.

"Yes," Gene said with effort. "It's just he responds like a couple of girls I got in the Galveston House."

The Kid straightened his face. "It's like holding one of those toy puppets."

They got him across Gus's shoulders, and Gus had him by an arm and a leg in front. Gus set his foot to the ladder climbing slowly, one foot up both feet on, and pulling at the railing with his free hand. With each step the Satchel Man's head dipped and thudded the railing.

Halfway up Gus stopped.

"What's happening?"

"Nothing," the Kid said. "Keep going."

Gus took another step.

Thud

"I said what's happening?"

"Keep going; you're nearly there."

Thud

Thud

"Damnit!"

"One more step, Gus."

Thud

"It was his head bumping, Gus."

"Well Jesus couldn't you —"

"I had to keep the leg cleared. Let's go on."

"No," Gus said. "Not until I get the head cleared." He hitched his shoulders until he got the head so he could hold it clear. Cupping the gray head in his hand he carried him to the Bosun's locker.

The Bosun sat on deck before the locker with canvas spilling his lap. He pulled the canvas toward him, and his shears spilled it evenly on either side.

They put the hatch board on deck and laid the Satchel Man on it.

When the Bosun's shears stopped, he fitted a sail maker's glove in his hand. "I guess nothing we ever learn becomes useless," he said and slipped the needle into the canvas.

"We've got to wash him," the Kid said.

"Yes," Gus said. "I'll get some buckets and washrags."

As the Kid began stripping the Satchel Man's skivvies, Gene said, "Wash him? In a little while he going to have the bath of his life, and he's never been too fond of water anyway. Can't you wait?"

"Hush. And close the open eye," the Bosun said.

"Those fish won't care if the eye's open or closed," the Fat Firemen said.

"I care. I don't want him to see how crooked my stitches have become, or maybe I don't want to look at it."

"I'll get him some clean clothes," the Kid said holding the skivvies between thumb and forefinger.

On his way aft he threw the skivvies over the side.

He didn't know what he expected to find in the Satchel Man's private locker, but what he found was not what he expected. He opened the unprotected locker feeling he was

looking into the Satchel Man's secret self. On the top shelf
sat the toilet articles: a razor, a comb, a cake of soap. In the
bottom were his work shoes, rubber boots, and work gloves.
His souwester and oilskins hung from a peg. Folded neatly
on a shelf were his extra pair of khakis, extra shirt, and extra
skivvies. Everything in the locker had been bought from the
ship's slopchest — except the thick, square billfold studded
and cornered in brass and hung with a brass belt chain.
The black leather was stamped in gold with a fouled anchor and beneath the anchor the words UNION MADE.

In spite of himself he opened the billfold. It contained in
fitted plastic compartments his seaman's papers and union
book and nothing more.

He was seized with loneliness. Bits of the Satchel Man's
hair stuck to the comb and razor. And for some reason he
did not understand he slipped the comb in his pocket, put
the razor in his own locker, and walked back to the Bosun's
locker.

From the railing he watched the flat becalmed surface of
the water merge and disappear into the horizonless sky.
The *Ekonk* was the only movement inside the blue bowl of
the world. The comb and razor were the only intimate
things in the Satchel Man's locker. He would use them and
remember.

Gus was washing the Satchel Man's feet when he came
with the clean clothes, and they were toweling him when
the Captain came. The Captain and the Chief Mate came
wearing their golden hats and blue coats with golden
sleeves. The Captain and Mate knelt on either side of the
Satchel Man stiffening on the board. They both felt
the Satchel Man's neck and his arms, and when they
rose the Captain turned to the Bosun. "He is dead," the
Captain said.

"Yessir," the Bosun said.

"I'm sorry," the Captain said, "but I had to make a formal declaration. How soon will you have him ready, Bosun?"

"Half an hour?" the Bosun said.

"Then we'll bury him in forty-five minutes." The Captain turned, swayed, caught his balance, and turned back. "Bosun, put in a link of anchor chain from the machine shop. Don't you think?"

"Yessir. That should be enough."

The Bosun slipped the needle and looked at the Fat Fireman. "Will you get the keys to the machine shop?"

Gene rubbed a palm over the veined translucent flesh of his stomach. "Hey, Fats, the Kid and I'll go with you. You're already carrying all you can carry."

The Fat Fireman mumbled an oath, then patted his belly with both hands. "You're just jealous. This ship ever goes down I'll live twice as long as you. You'd last maybe three weeks without food. I'd last three months."

"Ha," Gene said. "If the *Ekonk* ever goes down, she'll take you with her. It takes you thirty minutes to haul your belly out of the engine room. The only thing your belly does is put you two days ahead of the Satchel Man. You're prebloated."

When the Kid and Gene, carrying the sixty-pound link from the machine shop, came back with the Fat Fireman puffing behind them, Red and Gus were sliding the Satchel Man into the canvas bag. They were pulling the bag over his knaki shoulders when Gene said, "Wait," and pushed the chain link in and stuffed it down around the feet. Again they pulled the canvas over the shoulders and over his rigid chin when Gus said, "Wait." Gus pulled the canvas down and unbuttoned the khaki collar. "He never buttoned it,"

Gus explained. They pulled the canvas over his shoulders and half over his jutting nose when the Kid said, "Wait." He knelt beside the Satchel Man and with the comb smoothed the scraggled hair.

He searched the old face: thin lids covered marble eyes, the slightly open mouth held a tongue dry as a rock, the lump of jaw swelled the gray, stubbled beard out of shape, and the long-lobed ears stuck out inquisitively. He had never really looked at ears before — stuck on like afterthoughts. He smoothed the curves of stiff gray eyebrows, first the left, then the right.

"Now," he said.

They pulled the canvas across the rigid face and the Bosun slipped the needle above the head. The Satchel Man's nose bulged the canvas.

"I'm going up on deck," Gus said. "I need air."

"Me too," the Fat Fireman said.

Only the Kid and Gene and a shriveled electrician sat with the Bosun slipping the needle across the last opening.

"I like your stitches," the old Electrician said thoughtfully.

"They could be better. It's been a long time. You see the stitches, Kid? They should all be even and shaped alike, not for looks, but so they will all take the same pull. If one stitch is out of line or out of shape, it unevens the stress, and when one stitch breaks, they are all broken."

"Yessir."

The Bosun tied off. "It is done."

"Yes," the old Electrician said. "He is ready now."

They picked up the hatch board with the canvas bag at a balance, the Kid holding the front, Gene the back. The Kid led them to the railing beneath the bridge among the waiting crewmen standing in little groups, sitting on hatches, leaning over the railing. The crewmen saw them coming with the canvas body balanced to the board, and they all got to their feet. Putting his end of the board on the railing, the Kid stepped to help Gene. Gene shifted and they faced each other, hands clasped beneath the board.

The Captain stepped on deck and raised his eyes to the Mate leaning over the bridge. The Mate's head disappeared, and the *ring ring* of the telegraph bell hung the air. The *Ekonk's* thumping engine stopped, and the propeller stopped. The *Ekonk* sank at the head as she slid slowly on the mirror of water.

"Men," the Captain said standing with his golden hat under a golden arm holding a golden Bible. "We're here to bury our shipmate, Arthur James, Able-Bodied Seaman."

The crew scraped their feet and dragged off their caps. The Kid hitched the board, grabbed his black watch cap off, and quickly recaught Gene's hands. Standing between Gene and the Kid, the Captain read the Bible. None of the bareheaded crew heard the Captain's words, but all had trouble finding a place to look. The Bosun studied a spot of deck rust and began working at it with his toe. He scattered the rust and smoothed it. When he had it perfectly smooth with only a circle of rust color left in the steel, he suddenly groaned deeply and his eyes rose seaward.

The shriveled Electrician admired the stitches. His eyes followed the stitches up one side the canvas then he rose on tiptoe to follow them down the other. When he heard the Bosun's deep groan, he too looked seaward.

Red fixed his eyes where the horizon should be and stared until he believed he could see it.

Gene looked across the canvas body at the Kid's eyes and

thought how much the Kid resembled Aqua Velva — the moist skin, the silken lashes and eyebrows. It would be good getting back home. This trip would last him a long time. Aqua Velva. A groan filled his ears, and he groaned at the thought of her.

The Fat Fireman's eyes circled the rim of his stomach. *Prebloated.* By God, he wished the ship would go down. He'd show them. They'd all be left on a barren island, the whole crew. No, in a lifeboat, him and Gene and Slim the Oiler and the Kid and the Satchel Man — him and all the skinny ones. He'd keep them alive. They'd kneel at his stomach and suckle. He saw their heads nuzzle his stomach's rim and suck the fat from his flesh. He heard a deep groan and thinking the groan was his, he looked around to see if anyone had noticed.

The Captain's bent head followed the words in the golden book, but in his mind he saw himself telling this day to the Port Captain. *I buried a man this last trip.* Let the Port Captain try topping today with some business story. Hell. Most of them at their desks secretly envied the seagoing experience. At a deep groan, his voice faltered and his eyes lost their place.

The Cook watched the Captain, studied the way the Captain stood, the way he held the Bible, the way he read, his total aspect. He'd have to tell this one. It would really impress them. *I buried a man at sea this last trip.* He saw the Captain falter with emotion and lose his place. He must remember to practice faltering that way. It was very moving. The Cook's eyes teared.

The Kid found himself looking at the bulge of nose. He looked away and at the Captain. The Captain's nose hung long from his face with nose holes wide and vacant. He looked away from the Captain's nose and into the earhole opening the Captain's brain.

Holes. Holes all over his head. And, like worms, holes at the other end. The fish wouldn't be faster, only natural. His hands didn't hold the Satchel Man, they held food. The Satchel Man wasn't in his hands but in his head. The Satchel Man was a dream in his head just as those nights with her in the Ice Chest were a dream. For the rest of his life he would dream her and the Satchel Man. Then one day his dream would be put to sleep and he would sleep in the heads of other dreamers, indistinguishable, lost, no more no less than a night's forgotten dream. Forgotten, but there in the head all the same.

The Captain's hand touched theirs clasped beneath the board.

"All right, men."

Their hands raised.

The canvas body whispered against the board.

The emptiness of the board held him astonished, then he heard the splash, and they all crowded the railing.

The Satchel Man stood erect in the water.

The chain link at his feet stood him nodding stiffly erect in a halo of blue ripples. The Satchel Man nodded in blue circles away from the ship.

In silence they waited.

When the Satchel Man had floated fifty yards away, Red said, "I think he could of used another link."

"Hell no, Red, it ain't that," Gene said. "He's waiting for a wind."

"Hush," the Bosun said.

"No really," Gene protested. "Soon as a wind comes up he's heading out. He's going to pop up a little sail and — "

"Please," Gus said.

They waited.

They put their caps back on and leaned on the railing.

After a while the Kid said, "How long does it take, Boats?"

"I don't know. Do you know, Captain?"

"I don't know either."

The canvas body floated in the mirrored haze. It hung in the blue, no longer nodding or making circles. To the Kid it appeared to be floating in air.

"He looks to be going up instead of down," Red said.

"Hush," the Bosun said. "If you were out there looking here, we would appear to be floating in the air too."

"I know," Red said.

"He's taking his own sweet time," Gene said. "All those years he saved the steamship companies money by steering so straight, now he's taking a little of it back."

"We can wait," the Chief Mate said.

"I can do waiting," Blackie said. "Once I waited a long time in a place."

"Yes," Gus said. "You can do waiting, Blackie. Not many can."

"He's getting smaller," the Kid said.

"I can't see him," the Bosun said.

After a moment Gene said, "It's true. He's going down standing straight up."

They took off their caps.

"Where is he now?" the Bosun asked.

"He's fixing to dive," Red said. "Stern first."

The white canvas in the blue haze shortened and disappeared into the mix of air and water.

"Where is he now?" the Bosun asked.

"He's gone now," the Kid said.

The shriveled Electrician said, "He just stood there getting smaller until he disappeared."

Reluctantly they put their caps back on their heads and started walking aft, each man walking separate, alone with his thoughts.

When they were halfway aft, the engine started throbbing and the propeller thumping. The *Ekonk's* head raised to meet the water. They were underway again.

4

After dark the Kid paced the focslehead to watch bells ringing away the night. On the half-hour Gene rang the bell from the bridge, and he answered with the bell from the focslehead. Then he sang the lights. He did not think of the Satchel Man, he thought of time. Time grew inside him, and when it filled his chest with half an hour, Gene's bell rang the night and his answer joined Gene's in continuous rhythm.

"Lights are bright, sir."

Thank you.

How did he do it?

How did he know time without a watch or without looking at the stars? He guessed he knew it the way his mother's fingers knew the piano. He hadn't even known he could do it until one night he found himself, clapper in hand, looking impatiently at the bridge. For the first time his answering ring joined Gene's in continuous rhythm.

"Hey," Gene said that night after their watch was over, "you've learned to do it."

"Do what?"

"Tell time. You were waiting for my ring out there. Bet
you didn't know you were coming to sea to think in half-
hours."

"You can do it too?"

"No. But Red can, and the Satchel Man, and —"

The Satchel Man.

Tonight each time he'd reached for the clapper, he'd
felt the Satchel Man's ghostly hand there with his. The
Satchel Man had told the time with this bell. And when he
paced —

How many men had paced this deck on watch? How
many watches? How many ships? Suddenly the black
night closed around him. In spite of what the Bosun had
taught him about night vision, he stared into the center of
his eye, and darkness enclosed him. His pacing feet stumbled, and his balance left him. Swaying blindly, he reached
for something to hold and stumbled over a cleat. His hands
caught the railing. His eyes closed. Lights flashed inside
his head, so he opened his eyes and leaned into the blackness over the v of the bow. Who cared that the *Ekonk*'s signal lights were bright? Lights to signal what? Underway
for where?

He clicked the seashells in his pocket. She'd said the
ocean left them there when it made the mountains. Made
the mountains for what? Time moved, time swelled, time
turned the Satchel Man into mist. God, was he ever to be
burdened? Who cared if you lived to be a hundred and
turned into something good to eat, or that fish were faster?
Was this then it: this circle of flesh to flesh? He hadn't
needed to come all this way for that. He'd known *that*
shoveling manure for his mother's vegetable beds. God, to

be back in Joetown twining her long warmth with his, the two of them resting for a moment their lives against each other.

His eyes closed, and again lights lit the inside of his head.

His stomach turned sick with the warmth of her.

He held his hand in front of his face and opened his eyes. But he could not see his hand. It held no more substance than the Satchel Man's.

Deliberately he shook his head. He quit looking into the dark center of his eye. He looked instead as the Bosun had taught him. *In the night you cannot see a thing direct. You have to look with the sides of your eyes.*

His eyes widened, and he looked as he'd been taught. Again stars hung the night. And in the bottoms of his eyes lay the stars' watery reflections.

The light of each star fell to the water's flat surface in a long streak. Each streak plumb-lined to his feet. Slowly he turned full around. Every star in the heavens streaked the water directly to him.

And he stood with all lights ending at his feet until the full moon rose and silvered the becalmed ocean.

And later with his chest full of time, his hand closed on the clapper as Gene rang eight bells into the night.

He rang his bell in answer and sang the lights.

"Lights are bright, sir."

Thank you.

On his way aft he stopped at the railing and dropped the seashells over the side.

That night he slept a peaceful sleep, and he rose in the morning to pace the focslehead and ring the bells and sing the lights until dawn. Just before the sun came up he left the focslehead for coffee. He filled his cup in the messroom, and when he stepped back on deck, coffee cup in hand, he stopped. On one side of the ship it was day, on the other night.

On one side the becalmed ocean lay all in dark except for the silvery path of the full moon sitting exactly on the edge of the horizon. On the other horizon sat the rising sun. On that side the ocean was all afire. He stood without breathing, his left hand in night, his right hand in day.

Then in an instant the night side was gone, and it was full day.

And with the day came a breeze rippling the becalmed surface. By afternoon the ripples were waves, and for the rest of the trip the breeze blew the *Ekonk's* decks. It blew over them all the way back into port.

On the Bus

ON THE GREYHOUND BUS carrying him back home to the mountains, the Kid watched the sun reflect its colors from the asphalt. On his left orderly rows of corn stretched to the horizon. On his right a white farmhouse rode low in green-black fields of corn and soybeans. One more day and one more night and he'd be back in the mountains. It was almost over. He'd meant to tell the others goodby, especially the Bosun, but nobody had told him about a crew paying off.

The two soldiers and the girl in back of the bus broke into song again. Last night they'd had the whole busload singing through the night, and between songs last night the Grayhead now sleeping beside him had wanted to talk. "What'd you learn out there, young fellow?"

"Beg your pardon?"

"Out there on the ocean, what'd you learn?"

"Don't know as I could say."

"Try."

The Grayhead had been serious, had really expected to be told something that maybe he had somehow missed, something that would help.

Maybe he should have told him what lay at the end of the rainbow they'd seen yesterday. They'd seen it through the bus window. Its colors arced down to disappear into the pall hovering the approaching city.

That was something he'd learned: rainbows.

Hey, guys, look at me. I'm the fucking pot of gold.

The last he'd seen of Blackie, Blackie was sitting inside a jukebox. The crew with their pockets full of money had all gathered at the dockside bar to telephone for taxis into the city. Seabags and lockers were stacked everywhere. The taxis kept arriving and waiting outside with meters ticking while someone insisted on one more round. About dark Blackie crossed to their table, invited the Bosun outside, and Gus threw Blackie across the table into the jukebox where he sat bleeding among the lights and records.

They fled.

They all piled into the taxis and headed out, leaving Blackie to face the police and the bill for the damages.

He and Gene rode the same taxi, and Gene insisted they go to a place he knew. It turned out to be a whorehouse. He kept telling Gene he had to catch a bus, but the two girls kept ordering another half bottle of champagne, and when he came downstairs with bursting head the next morning he had only three twenties left from his payoff. With his seabag over his shoulder he set out looking for the bus station.

He shouldered the seabag for over two hours. By the time he found the bus station his head was cleared. He boarded the bus with the seabag, a bottle of Pepsi, a sack of Hershey bars, an empty billfold, and promptly fell asleep.

That afternoon he woke up, sipped the Pepsi, and watched the rainbow disappear into the city's pall.

Hey guys, look at me, everybody!

"Hey, look at Blackie," the Mate on the bridge called. And the Cook sitting beneath a canopy cutting vegetables into his apron hollered aft, "Hey everybody, look at Blackie."

Blackie came down the deck inside the end of a rainbow. The *Ekonk* had sailed under the rainbow's foot, and Blackie had stepped inside it. With arms outstretched he pranced inside the shimmering colors.

Hey everybody, look at me!

Beads of colored moisture floated around him and covered him in bands of blue, and red, and pink, and violet, and yellow.

Look, look.

Blackie laughed and waved.

I'm the fucking pot of gold!

So he'd learned rainbows that day.

He propped his knees on the seat in front as the voices in back sang of love. He laughed and settled deeper into the seat. Blood throbbed his shoulders, and ahead asphalt particles sparkled the furnace colors of the sun.

It wouldn't take long.

The others would all be back out there soon, on another *Ekonk*.

Wherever he went, they'd be out there tending the ship's needs, watching the fires, ringing the bells and singing the lights, holding the ship steady, pushing water.

The fucking pot of gold.

On course.

He'd gone to sea to find the strongest thing in the world, and he had found it. But its empty shell had been lying there on the mountaintop all the time. He'd only needed the eye to see.